BRAVE AND BOLD!

Female DC Super Heroes Take On the Universe

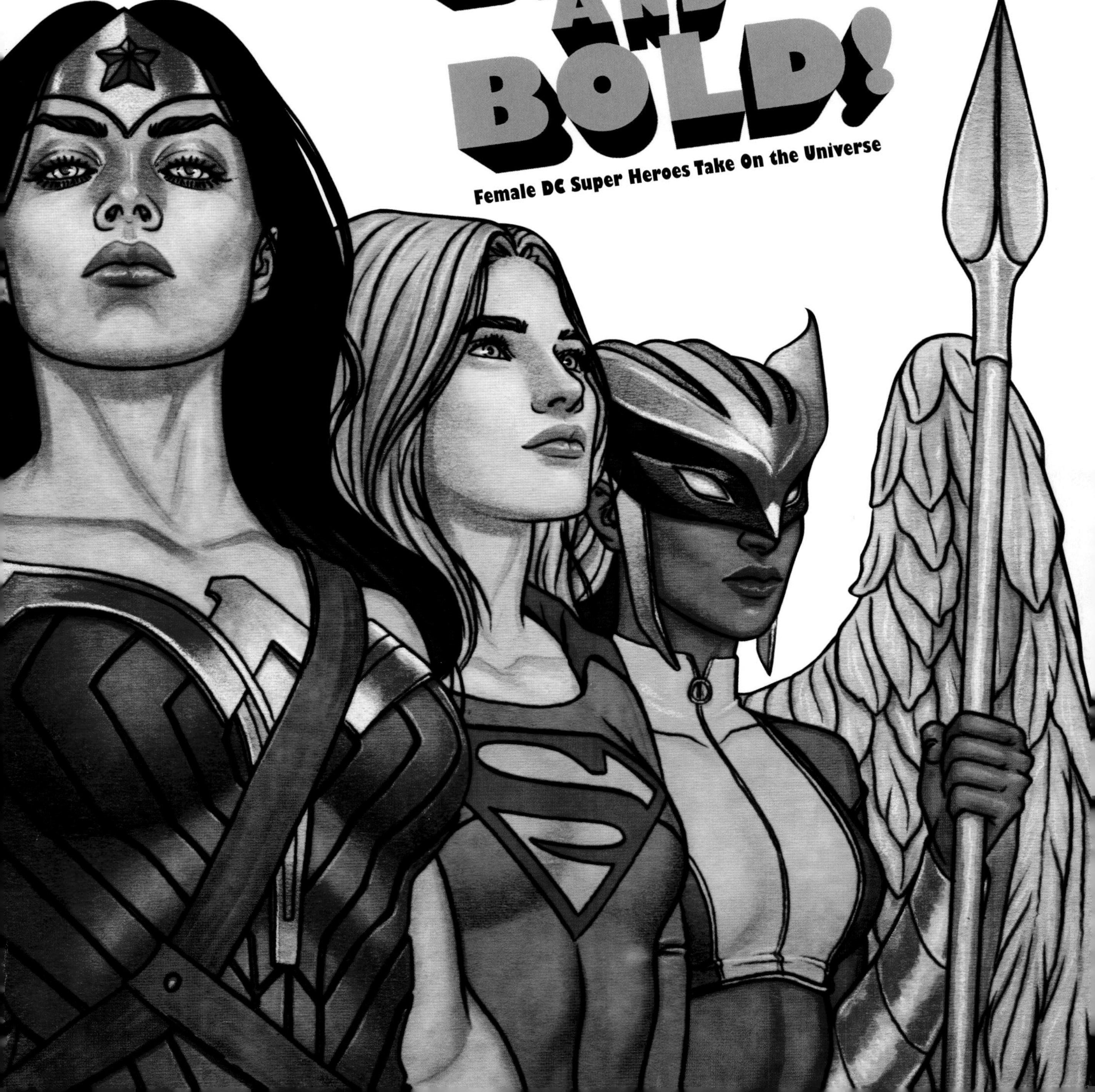

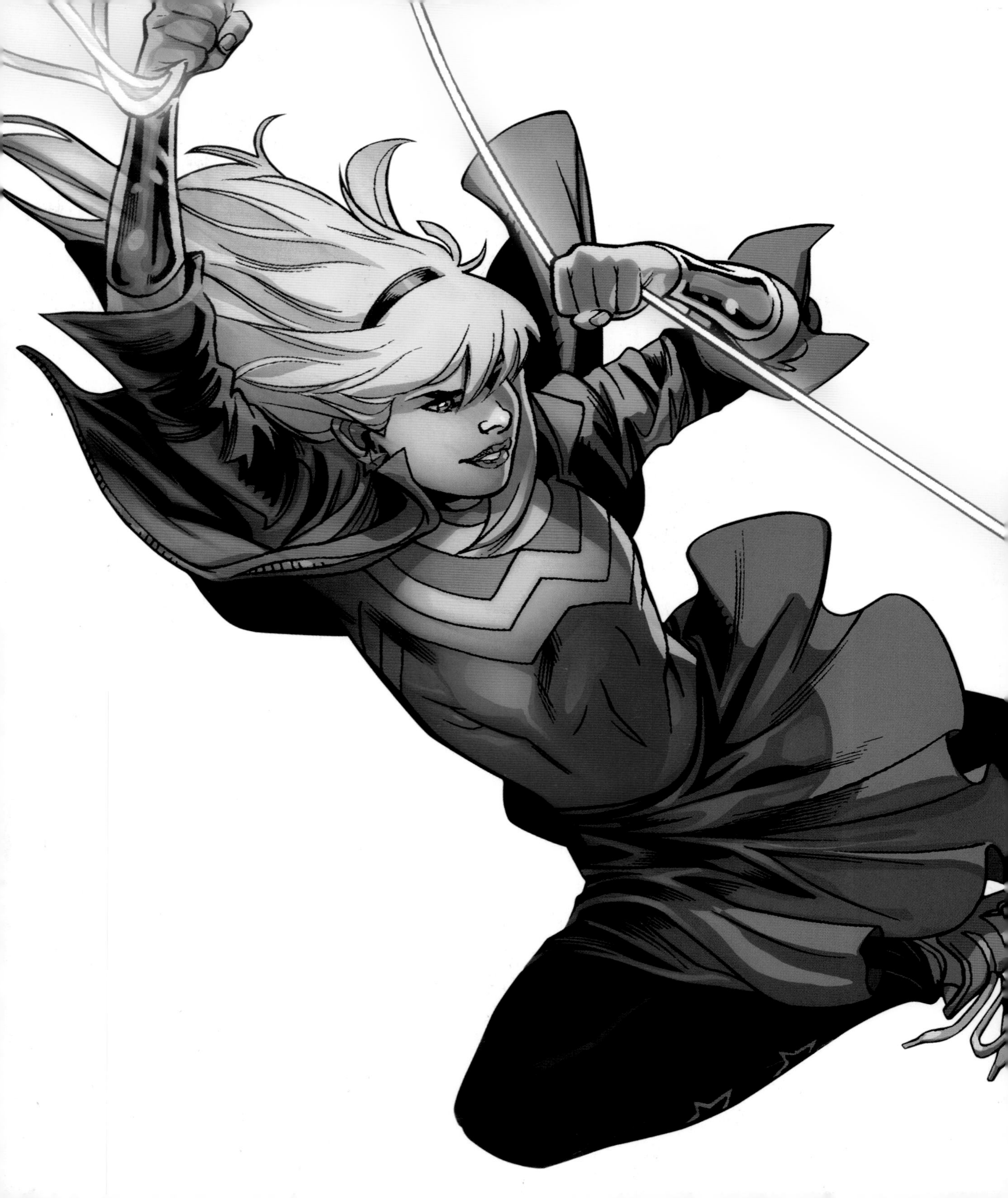

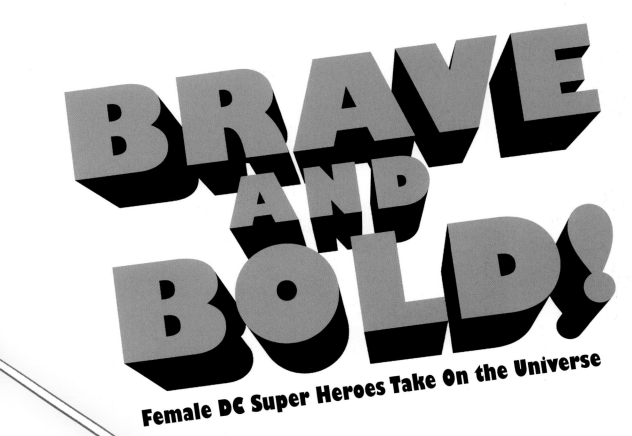

BRAVE AND BOLD!

Female DC Super Heroes Take On the Universe

Written by
Sam Maggs

CONTENTS

FOREWORD

As a little girl, I lived on a very remote farm. I was the only kid in my school with red hair, which I got teased about a lot. Because I was alone so often, I found myself drawn to reading, specifically to tales of adventure. But in all those stories, the girl characters were always having their adventures by accident, by falling down a rabbit hole or into a tornado.

One day, at a garage sale with my mother, I saw a stack of comics, and the book on top had Wonder Woman on the cover. I had no idea women could be Super Heroes, but here was Princess Diana, fierce as the sun. I must have read that comic a hundred times.

Later, I'd discover Batgirl, who was the smartest hero in Gotham City. Better yet, she had red hair! I remember going to school the next day, standing a little taller, raising my hand more in class. Because that's what Batgirl would have done.

Now I make comics for a living, writing about these same amazing women. I travel around the world talking about comics, meeting people from Singapore to Spain who love these characters just as much as I do. I've met girls who learned martial arts because of Black Canary, who fought cancer with Supergirl at their side. I met an astronaut who chose that career because Wonder Woman gave her courage.

I was once asked to give a keynote speech at the White House. I was pretty scared about it, until several staffers came up to show me they were wearing DC female Super Hero socks and ties under their business suits. Turns out everyone needs a little extra courage sometimes.

I'm proud of having worked on many of the characters in this beautiful book, each so perfectly encapsulated by Sam Maggs. I feel that they represent the greatest collection of fictional female heroes anywhere, from Lois Lane to Huntress, and their number keeps growing as more and more female creators and readers discover these amazing stories.

I hope they inspire you as they have me, as they have so many others of all ages and genders. I hope that getting this peek into their lives makes you, too, COMPASSIONATE, BOLD, CURIOUS, and PERSISTENT.

Because, from Gotham City to Themyscira to the depths of space to your hometown, the world will always need heroes!

Gail Simone, comic book writer

DC COMICS
THE NEW 52!
#1
$2.99
BATGIRL
SIMONE
SYAF
CIFUENTES
DC
Wonder Woman
25
GAIL
SIMONE
CHANG
DC
BIRDS of PREY
BLOOD AND CIRCUITS
GAIL SIMONE • NICOLA SCOTT • PAULO SIQUEIRA • JAMES RAIZ

Comic books written by Gail

INTRODUCTION

In a universe filled with adventure and danger, the brave female Super Heroes of DC's comic books change the world and shape the future. These girls and women come from different backgrounds and beginnings; some of them possess superpowers and others do not—but all take on the universe and triumph. Working on their own or together, female heroes fight for others, struggle through difficult times, smash down barriers—and prove their greatness time and time again.

To help readers navigate this book, the characters are arranged into four chapters relating to personal qualities: compassion, boldness, curiosity, and persistence. Each character may possess a combination, or all, of these qualities; the chapter they appear in indicates that they are a particularly good example of that strength.

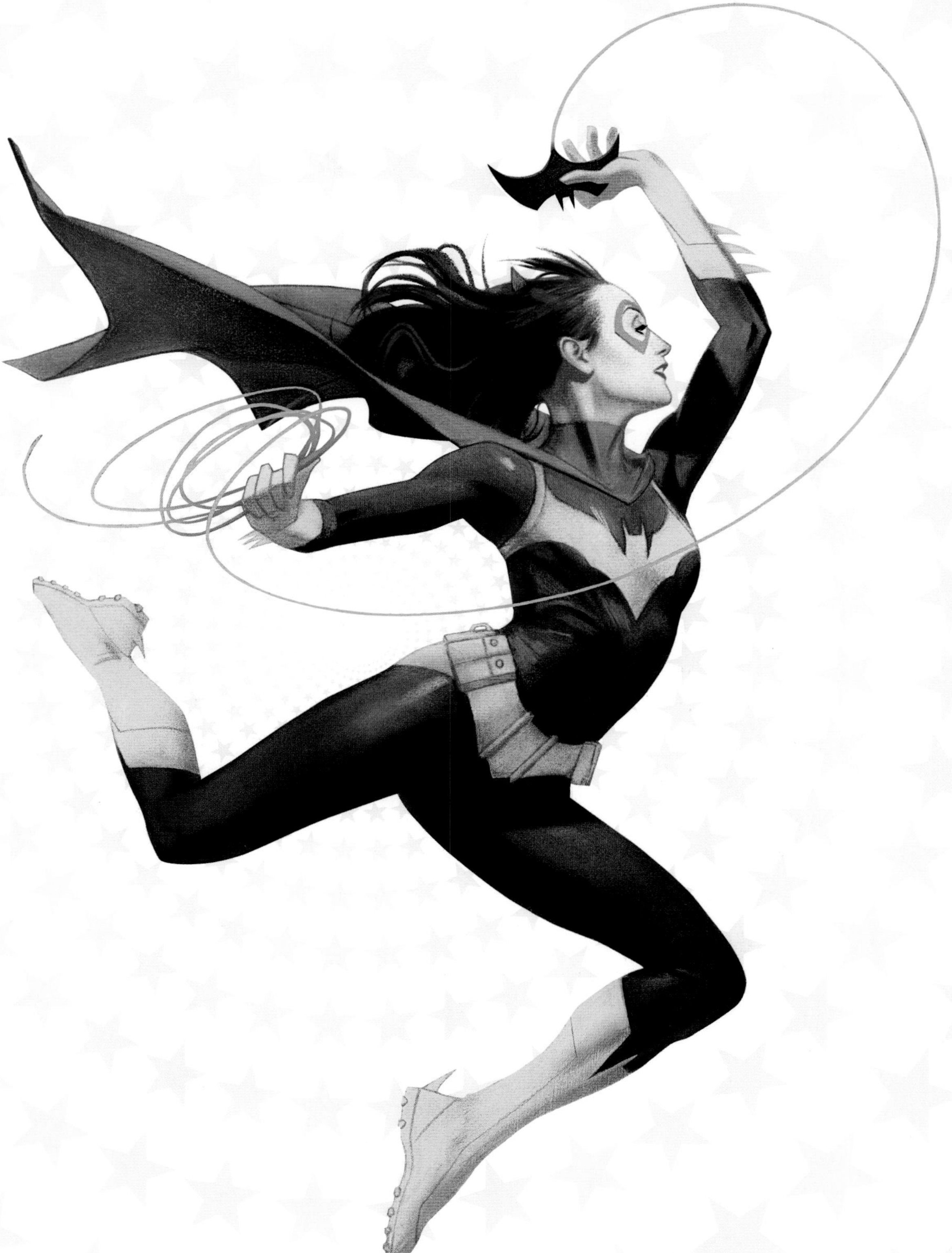

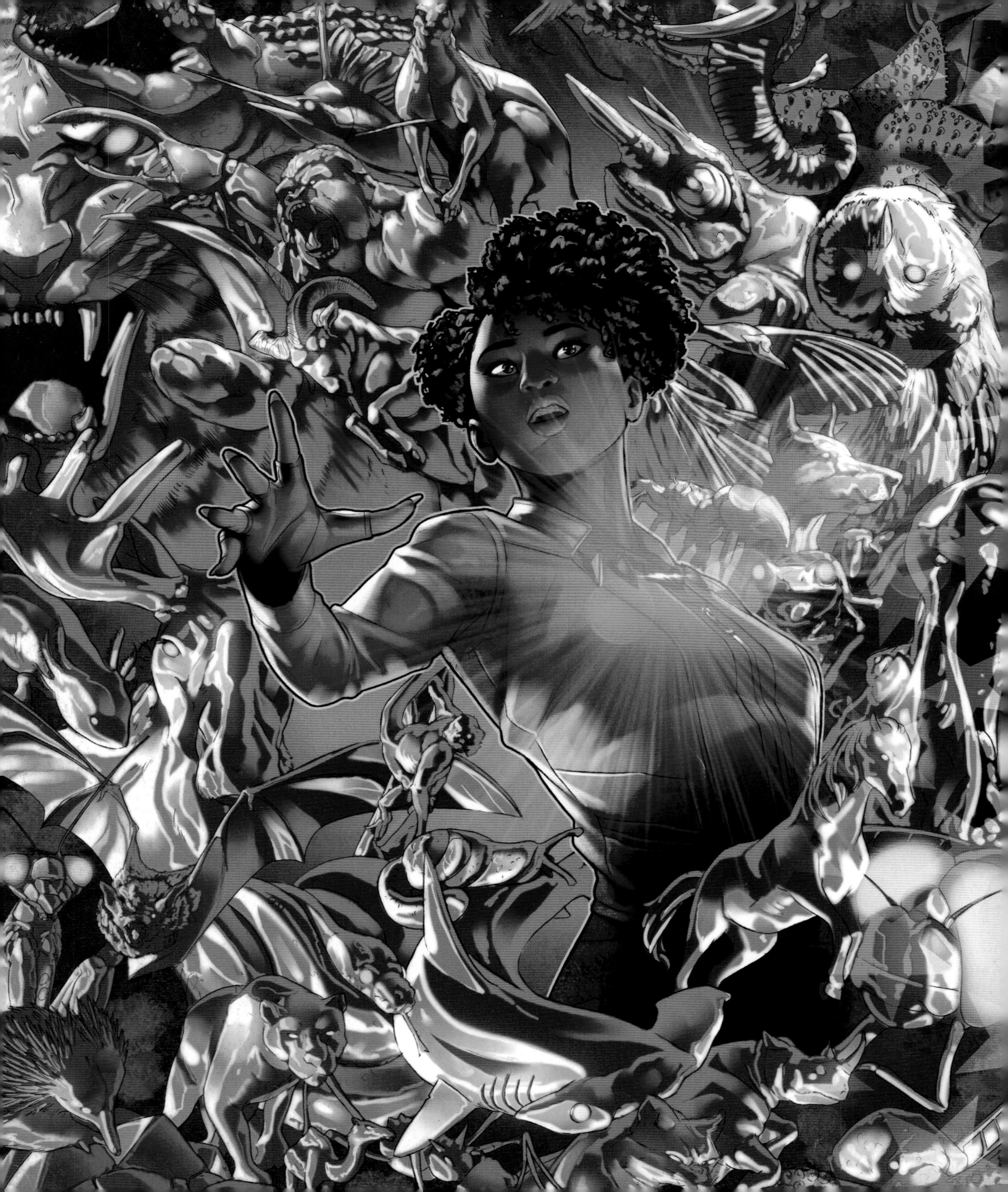

COMPASSIONATE

In troubled times, the most noble thing in the
world is to care about others. Brave, kind heroes such as
Wonder Woman and Vixen show their strength and willpower
by defending their allies and spreading messages of peace
and unity across the universe. These Super Heroes would
do anything to protect the ones they love.

◀ Vixen (p14)

WONDER WOMAN

"Love! Hatred won't win this—violence—but love just might!"

Born on the island paradise of Themyscira, Diana is the only heir of Hippolyta, queen of the immortal Amazon warriors. Diana was educated in art and literature, and highly trained in the use of weapons. She felt happy on the island, but she was also fascinated by humans and the outside world. When an American man crash-landed on Themyscira, Diana volunteered to return with him to his world. There, she could spread the Amazons' message of peace. Before her journey, Diana was given bulletproof bracelets and the Lasso of Truth. The Lasso forces anyone who touches the rope to be completely truthful.

After traveling with the man to America, Diana was visited by the Greek gods. They granted her super-strength, speed, durability, empathy, and flight. Unable to return to Themyscira without unleashing an evil god, Diana dedicated herself to protecting mortals. She prefers to solve problems peacefully and with kindness rather than violence. Named Wonder Woman by journalists impressed with her heroism, she will never stop fighting for truth and justice.

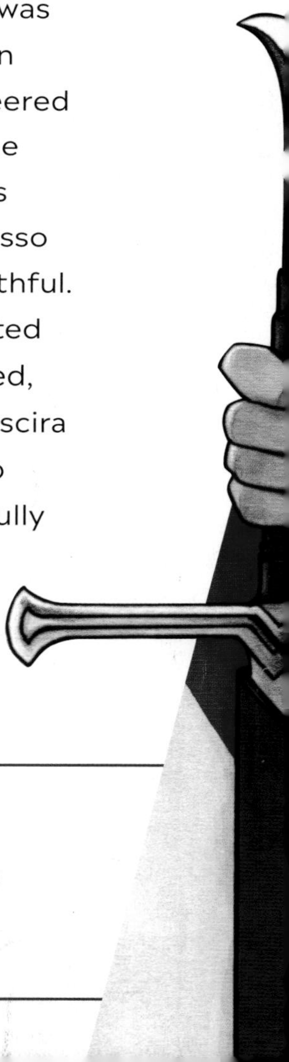

DATA FILE

Friends and allies: Etta Candy (p38), Donna Troy (p62)

Occupations: Adventurer, ambassador

Base: Washington, D.C.

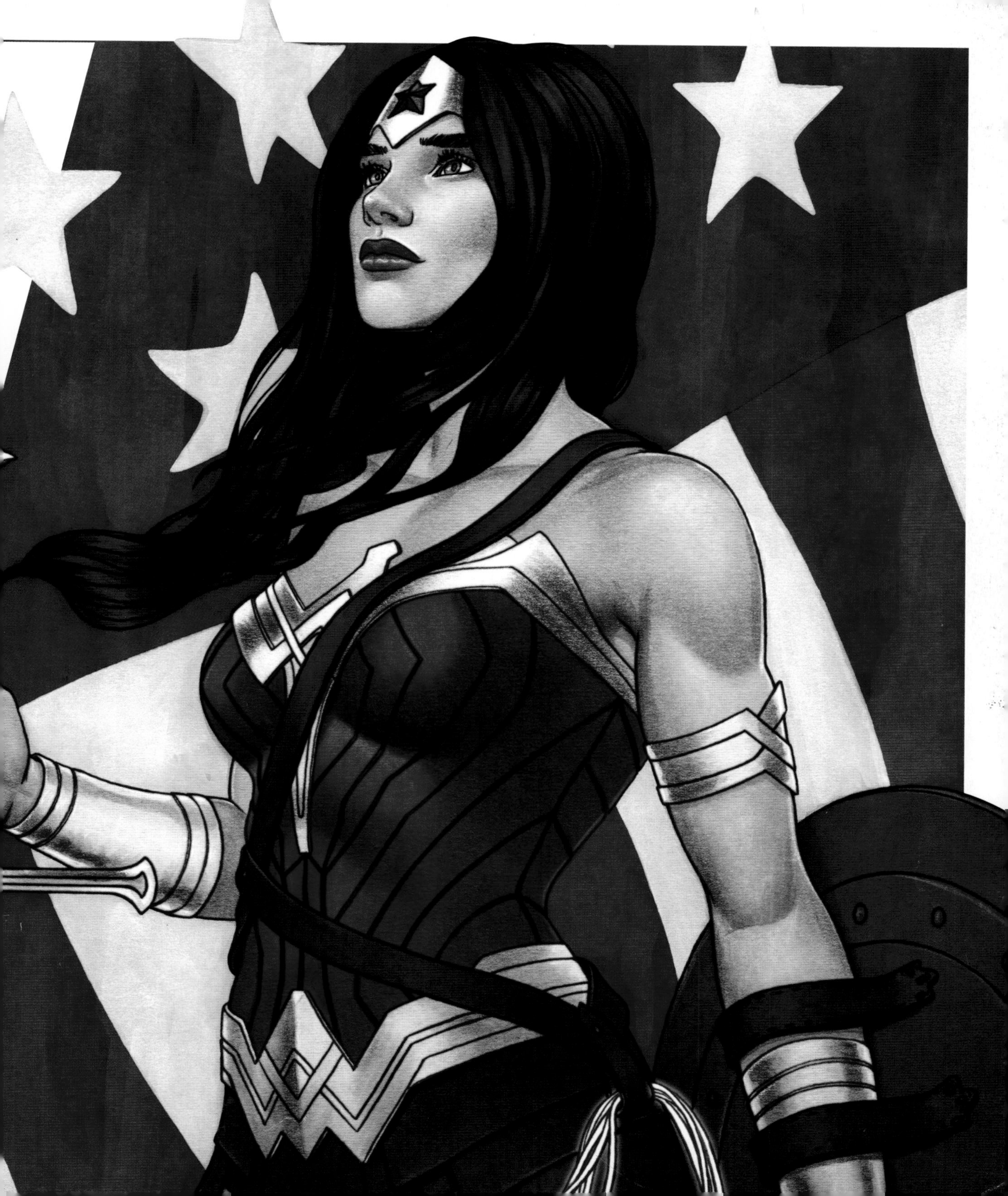

VIXEN

"I have many **families.** Many **names.** I am a **lion** of many **prides.**"

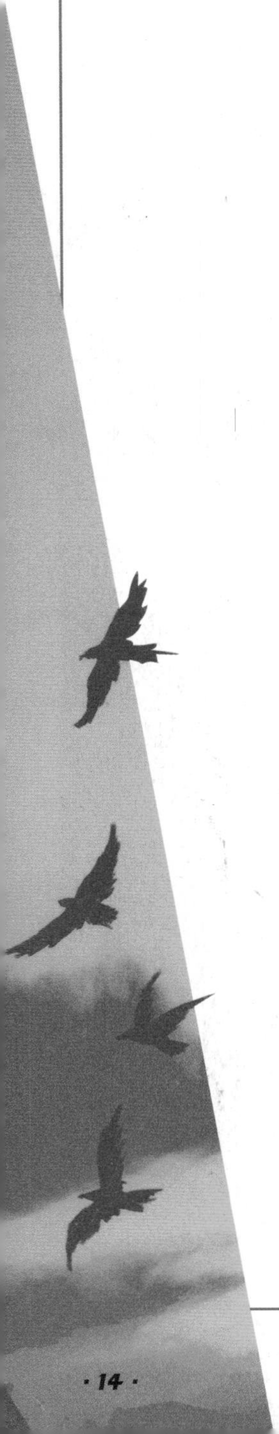

Mari McCabe was born in a small African village. She was gifted a valuable family heirloom, the Tantu Totem, by her father. The Totem was passed down by their ancestors in ancient Ghana. Mari uses the Totem to harness the power of any animal in the world through a link to The Red—a force that connects all life in the universe. The bearer of the Totem must use its powers to defend the innocent.

Mari moved to New York City and protects both her new home and the world as the Super Hero Vixen. With the Totem, Mari is able to take on the attributes of any animal. She can fly like a bird, grow claws like a cheetah, or see long distances like a hawk. Mari's strong, animal-like senses make her an incredible investigator. She has also worked as a model, an animal rights activist, a reality show star, and a business owner. This graceful, independent, and confident woman is a founder of the most recent version of the Justice League of America team. Alongside her teammates, including Frost, Vixen has helped defend New York City from extra-dimensional threats.

DATA FILE

Friends and allies: Black Canary (p16), Zatanna (p60)

Place of birth: Zambesi, Africa

Loves: All animals, some people

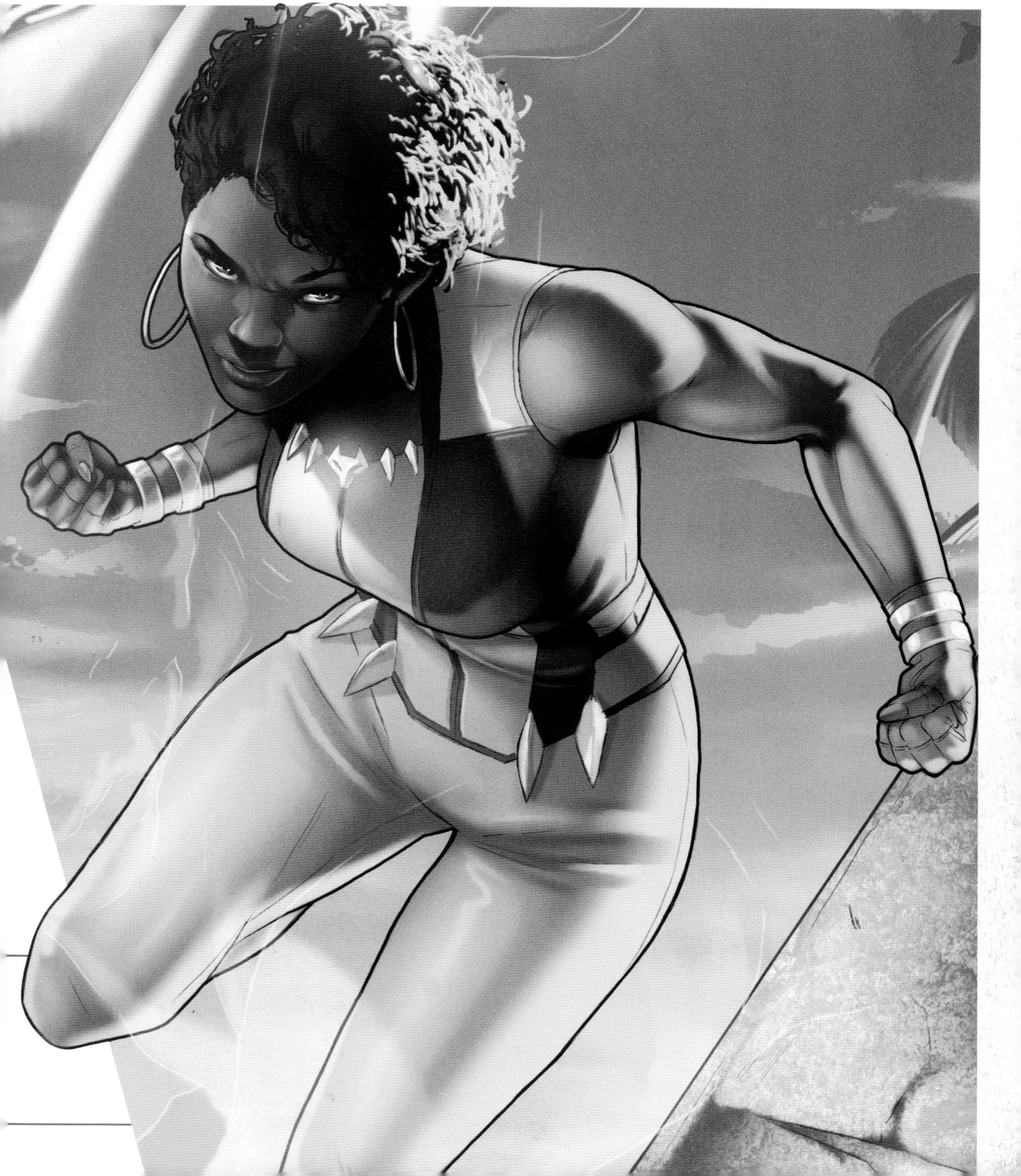

BLACK CANARY

"Get ready to scream for... Black Canary!"

By night, Dinah Drake is a rockstar, leading a band called Black Canary. By day, she is a crime fighter called the Black Canary, born with a supersonic scream. Her cry is so powerful that it can stun humans and destroy objects, depending on how close she is to them at the time. Fortunately, Dinah is not affected by her own cry, or by the effects of other loud noises.

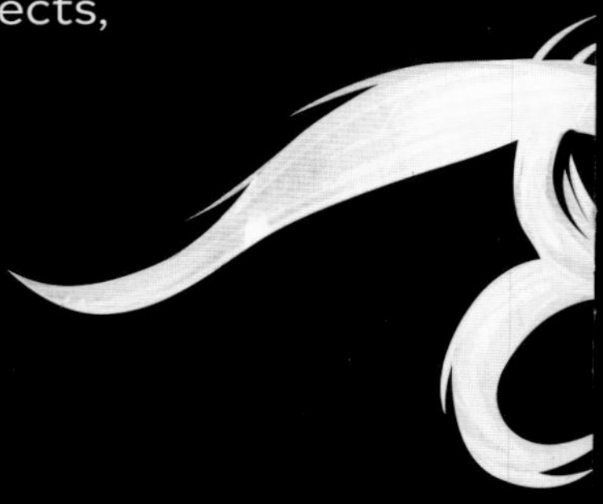

As a child, Dinah ran away from foster care. She grew up in her neighborhood dojo (a school for martial arts), learning many different forms of hand-to-hand combat, like boxing, Krav Maga, and jiujitsu. She found herself drawn to the world of spywork, teaming up with the Super Hero archer Green Arrow. Dinah later became the leader of the Birds of Prey team. She often wears a cool outfit including a leather jacket with a bird pictured on the back. Her rock concerts are always exciting, whether she happens to be fighting evil at the time or not.

DATA FILE

Friends and allies: Huntress (p40), Batgirl (p72), Orphan (p112)

Place of birth: Gotham City

Special skills: Fluent in French and Japanese

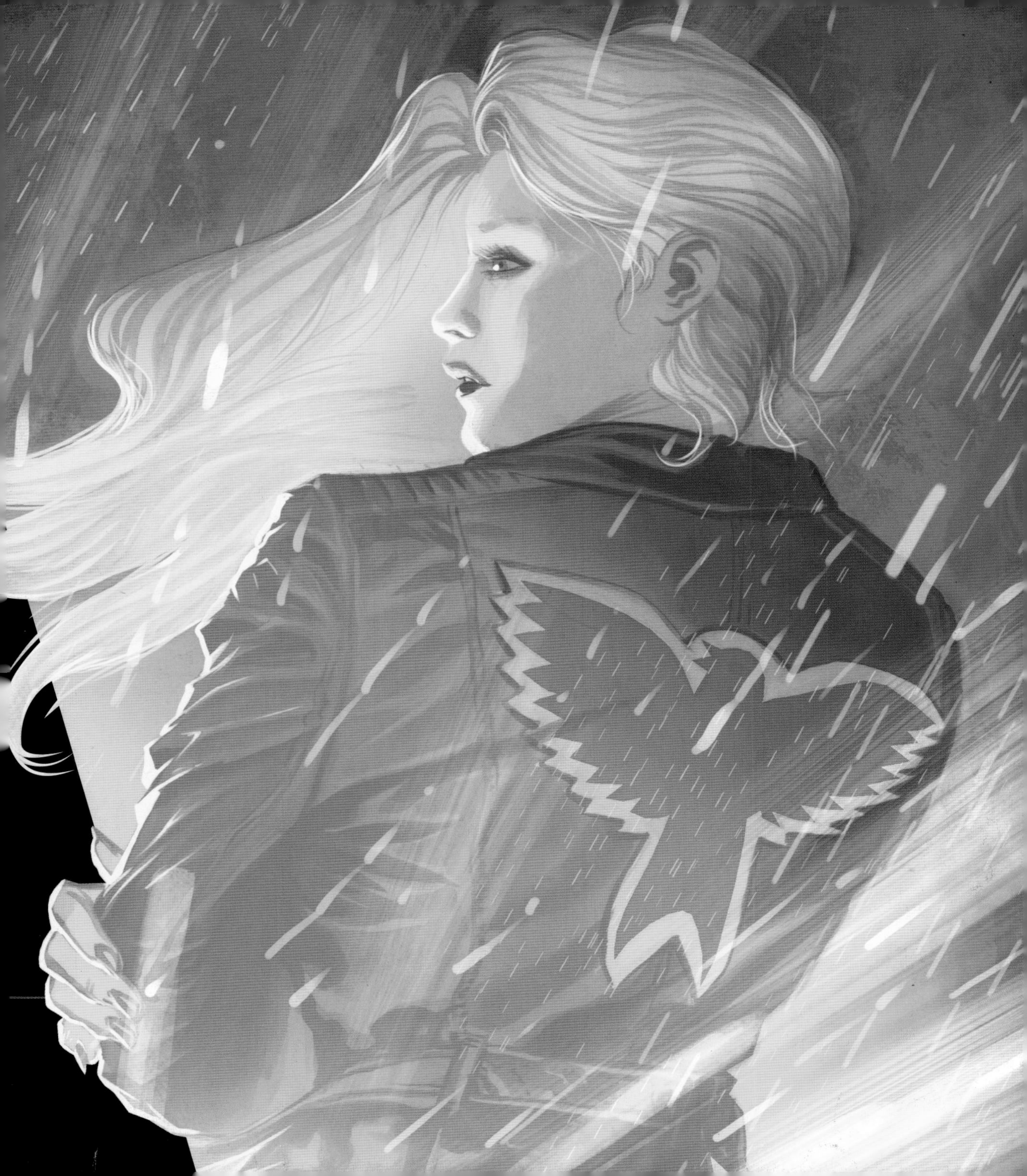

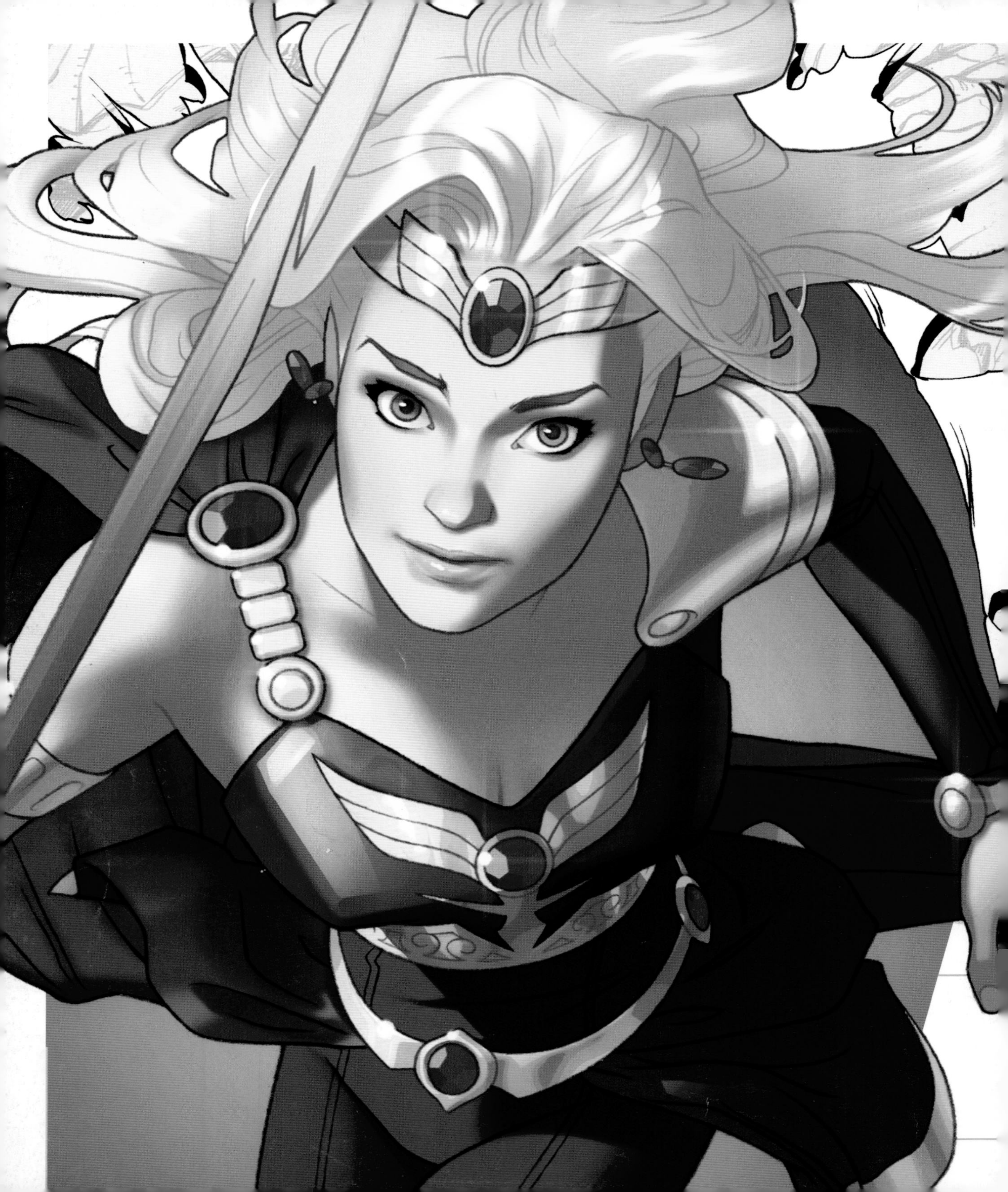

AMETHYST

"Lady, the only thing that brought me to Chicago was the best deep-dish pizza in the world."

Amaya is the heir to the royal House of Amethyst. In her home dimension of Gemworld people use crystals and gemstones to practice magic. As the most powerful magic user in Gemworld, Princess Amaya is able to manipulate light into hard crystals with her mind. She can create weapons of amethyst like daggers and claws. Amaya can also enhance gems, giving them powers like the ability to heal.

Amaya's mother brought her to Earth as a child to protect her from the evil plots of untrustworthy family members. She was raised near Chicago as Amy Winston, a regular girl. Her mother revealed the truth about Amaya's heritage when she turned 13 and trained her in gem magic. Amaya joined the magical Justice League Dark team as the Super Hero Amethyst. She is now a member of the Young Justice team of teenage Super Heroes. Amaya is graceful and kind and will sacrifice much for the good of others. She has amazing purple eyes.

DATA FILE

Friends and allies: Zatanna (p60), Wonder Girl (p66)
Place of birth: Nilaa, Gemworld
Occupations: Princess, student

DOVE

"You want our **strength?** You want our **hope?** You want our **fear?** You want our **rage? COME AND TAKE IT!**"

Dawn Granger is half of the team Hawk and Dove. Her crime-fighting and romantic partner, Hank Hall, is Hawk. He is the bringer of war, and his talents lie in deadly, aggressive attacks. Dawn is Dove, the bringer of peace. She is skilled at logic, plans, and defense. She can also fly and sense danger. Hawk and Dove's roles in this world were given to them by the Lords of Order and Chaos. These supernatural beings are responsible for the opposing forces in the universe.

For a brief time, Dawn's sister Holly gained the powers of Chaos and took on the role of Hawk. Though they often argued, Dawn and Holly worked together as members of the Teen Titans group until Holly's tragic death. Dawn has also been a member of the Birds of Prey team. Highly intelligent and compassionate, Dawn will always search for a peaceful solution to a quarrel before she enters a fight.

DATA FILE

Friends and allies: Lady Blackhawk (p46), Raven (p110)
Occupation: Georgetown College student
Enemies: Swan, Hunter

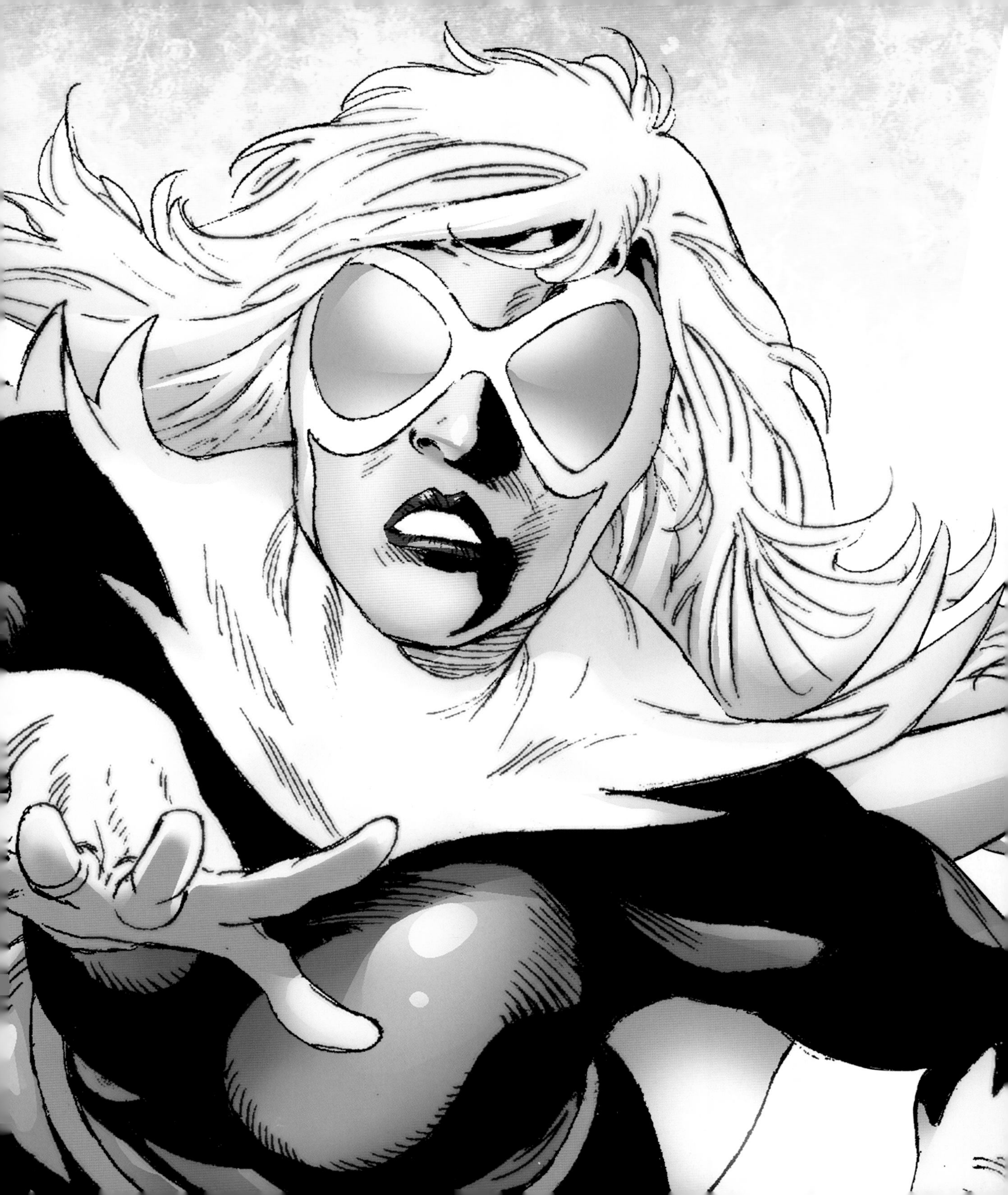

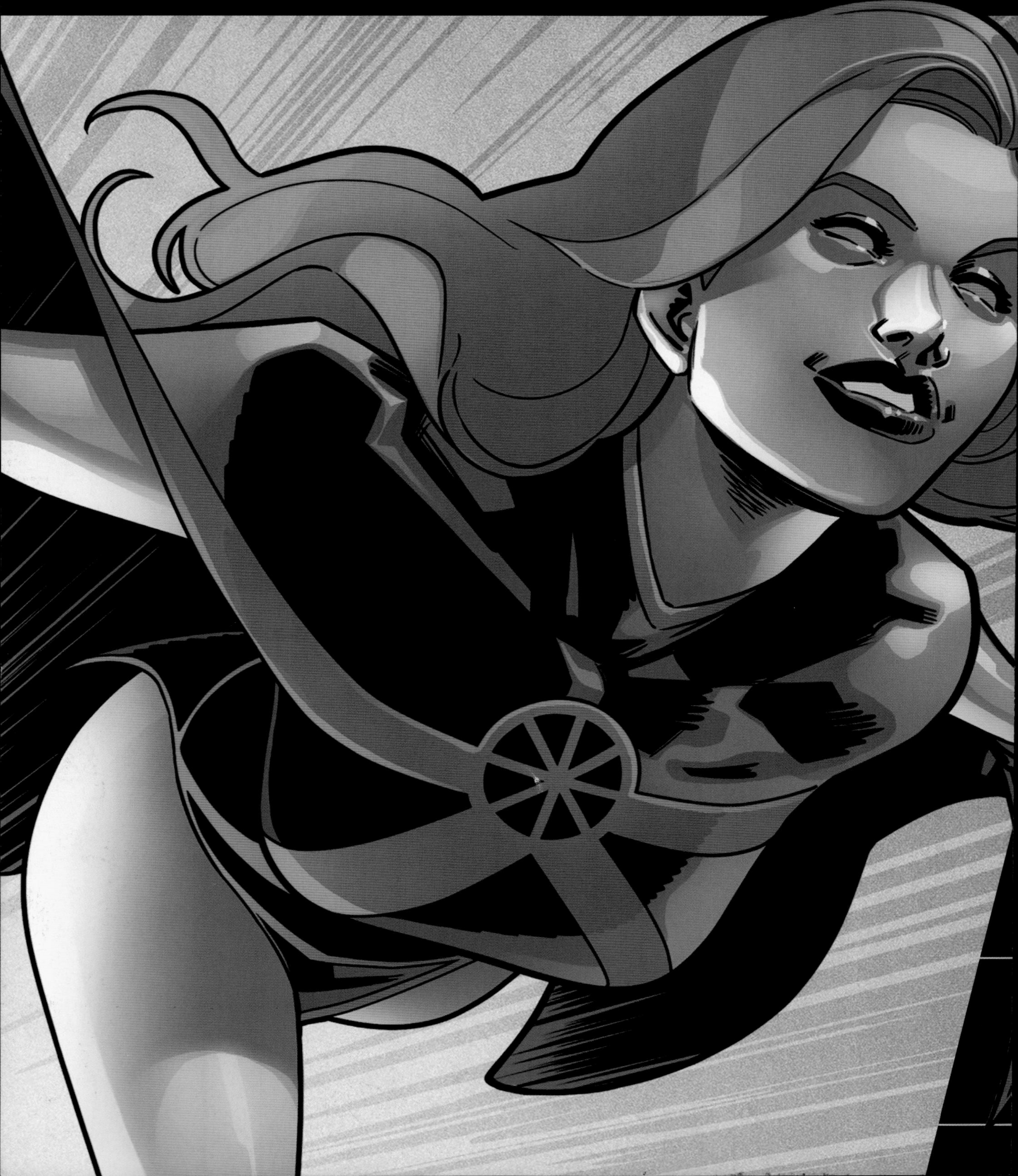

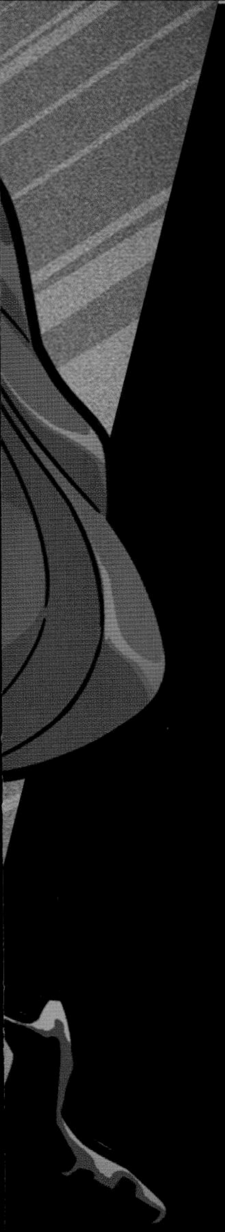

MISS MARTIAN

"You all assume I am alien and do not feel. Well, I feel."

M'gann M'orzz is a White Martian, a shape-shifter from Mars. She was born white-skinned and bald with four arms and a tail. The planet's violent White Martians and peaceful Green Martians were locked in a deadly civil war from which M'gann and her parents escaped and fled to Earth. There, M'gann was afraid of rejection by others due to White Martians' evil reputation. She changed her appearance and pretended to be a Green Martian like her uncle, the heroic Martian Manhunter.

M'gann attends high school as Megan Morse, the name of a character on her favorite TV show. She fights crime with the Teen Titans as Miss Martian. M'gann can fly, read minds, regenerate herself, shoot energy rays from her eyes, and move objects with her thoughts. Like all Martians, she is afraid of fire. M'gann has revealed her true nature as a White Martian to the other Titans, who have accepted her. Miss Martian does not understand many Earth customs, and spends as much time as she can in the Australian Outback. It reminds her of Mars.

DATA FILE

Friends and allies: Dove (p20), Donna Troy (p62)
Place of birth: Ma'aleca'andra (Mars)
Loves: Television, her Titan friends

SATURN GIRL

"I have peered into the **minds** of those that **hold onto hate** and I have seen the potential to **change that.**"

Irma Ardeen was born in the 30th century on Titan, Saturn's largest moon. Although all people from Titan have telekinetic powers—the ability to move objects with their minds—Irma was particularly talented. She trained hard and left home to join Earth's military branch, the Science Police. On the transport ship to Earth, Irma helped two boys prevent an assassination attempt. Together, they decided to form the Legion of Super-Heroes, a team of teenage crime fighters. She took on the Super Hero name Saturn Girl.

Irma became the Legion's leader. She later married her Legion cofounder, Lightning Lad, and they had twin sons. She has traveled back to the 20th and 21st centuries many times to help defeat evil from her past. Irma is known for her kind heart and willingness to help those in need. Her special Legion Flight Ring protects her while flying through space. Irma wears a pink or red jumpsuit with a picture of Saturn on it.

DATA FILE

Friends and allies: Supergirl (p32), Phantom Girl (p122)
Base: Legion Headquarters, Metropolis
Loves: Laser guns, leadership

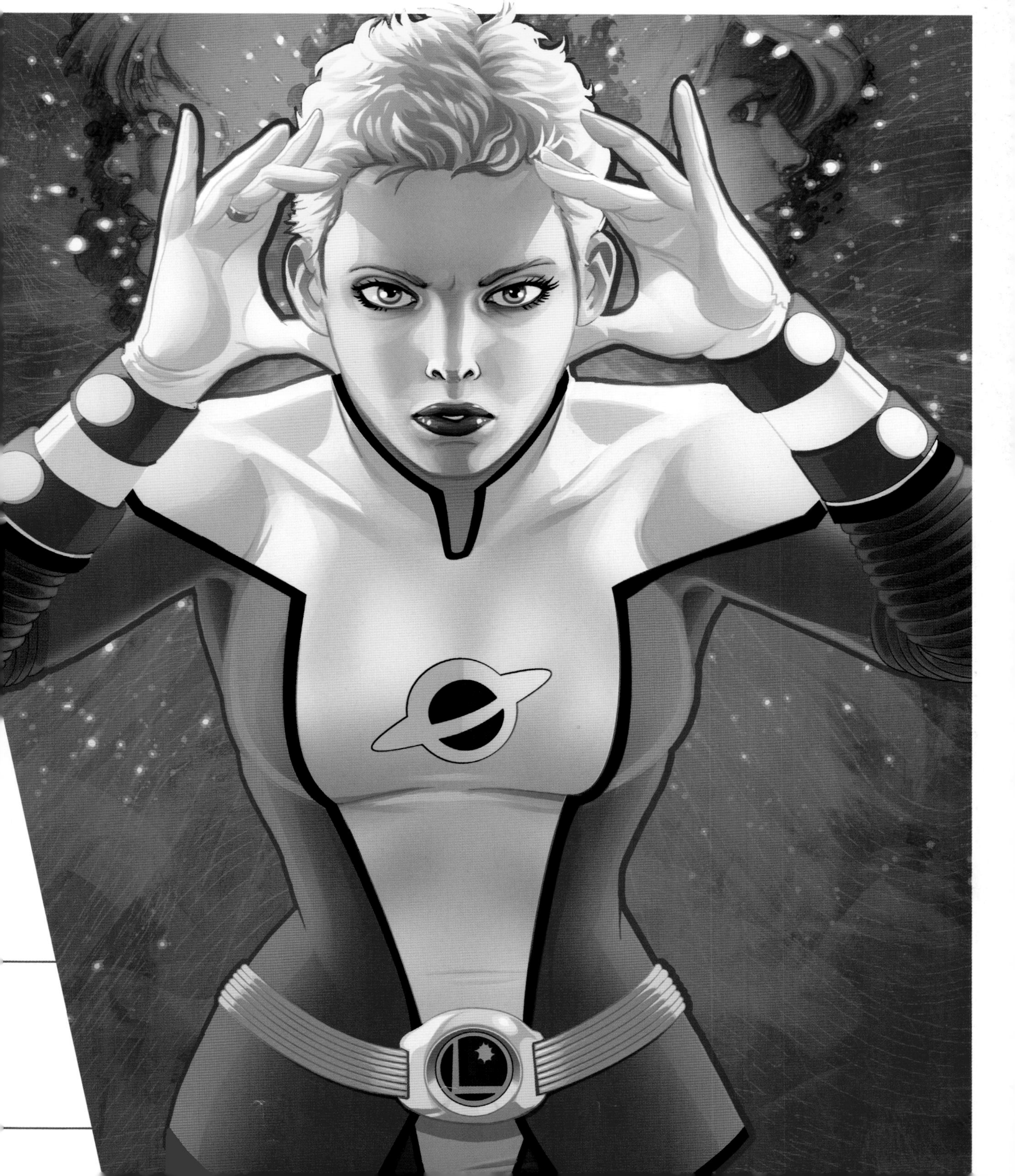

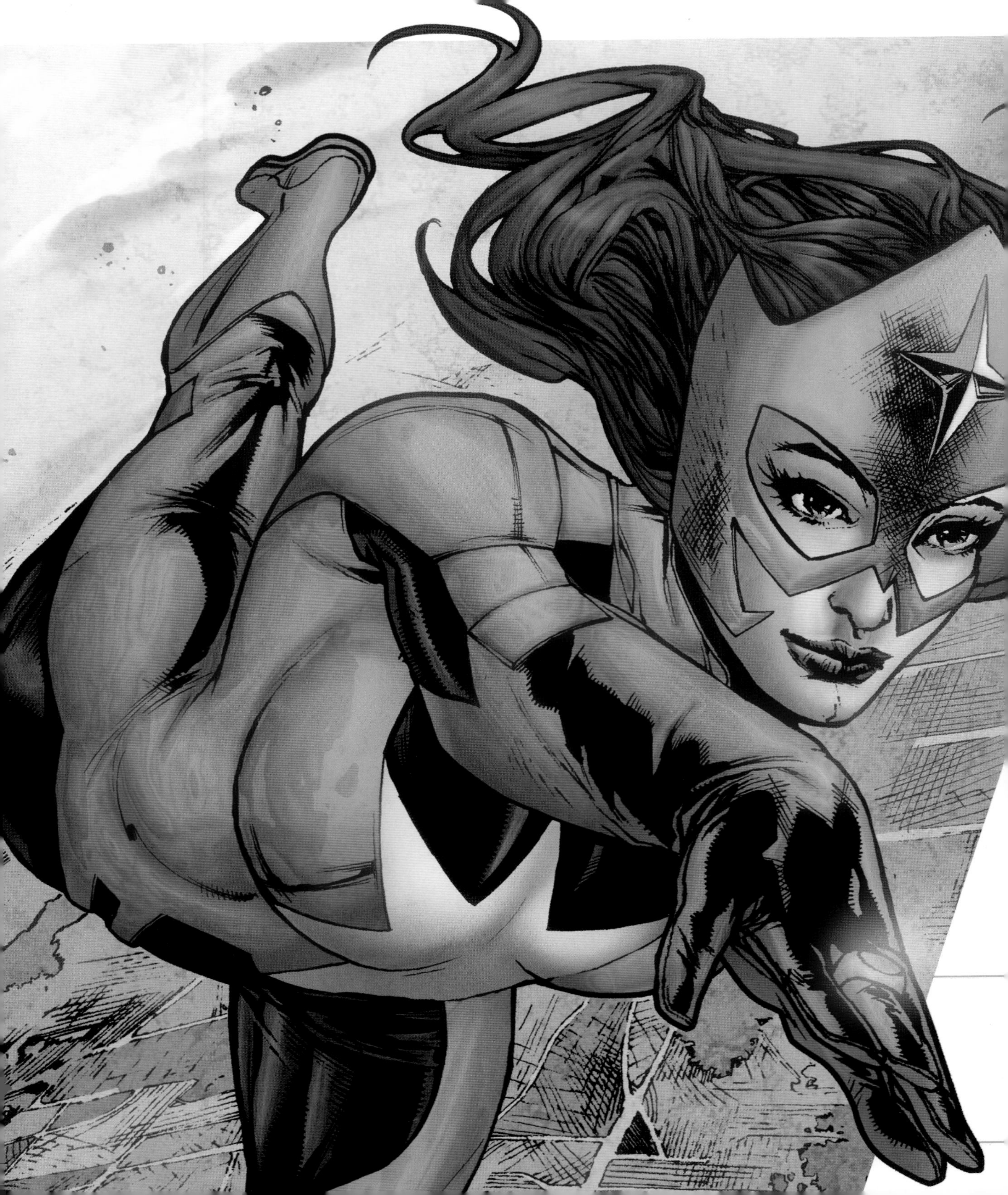

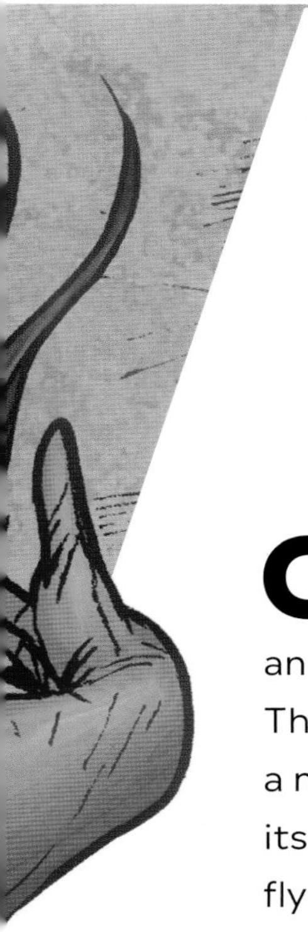

STAR SAPPHIRE

"Love is beautiful. Love is inspiring. But love is also lethal."

Carol Ferris was a pilot and the boss of her family's aviation company. She was shocked when she was selected by an alien race called the Zamarons to be their newest leader. The Zamarons named Carol the Star Sapphire and gave her a magical gemstone ring. This Star Sapphire power ring grants its user control over the violet energy of love. Its wearer can fly and manipulate energy. Carol's ring can also teleport her directly to the person she loves most.

The Zamarons have sent out other Star Sapphire power rings to women capable of great love. Though the ring tried at first to control Carol's mind and tempt her toward evil, she conquered it with her strong willpower and caring heart. The women of the Star Sapphire (or Violet Lantern) Corps now protect love across the universe by fighting against the forces of evil. As Star Sapphire, Carol can heal wounds and even bring the dead back to life, reuniting them with beloved family members.

DATA FILE

Friends and allies: Soranik Natu (p90), Green Lantern (p98)

Occupations: Aviator, businesswoman

Base: Coast City, CA

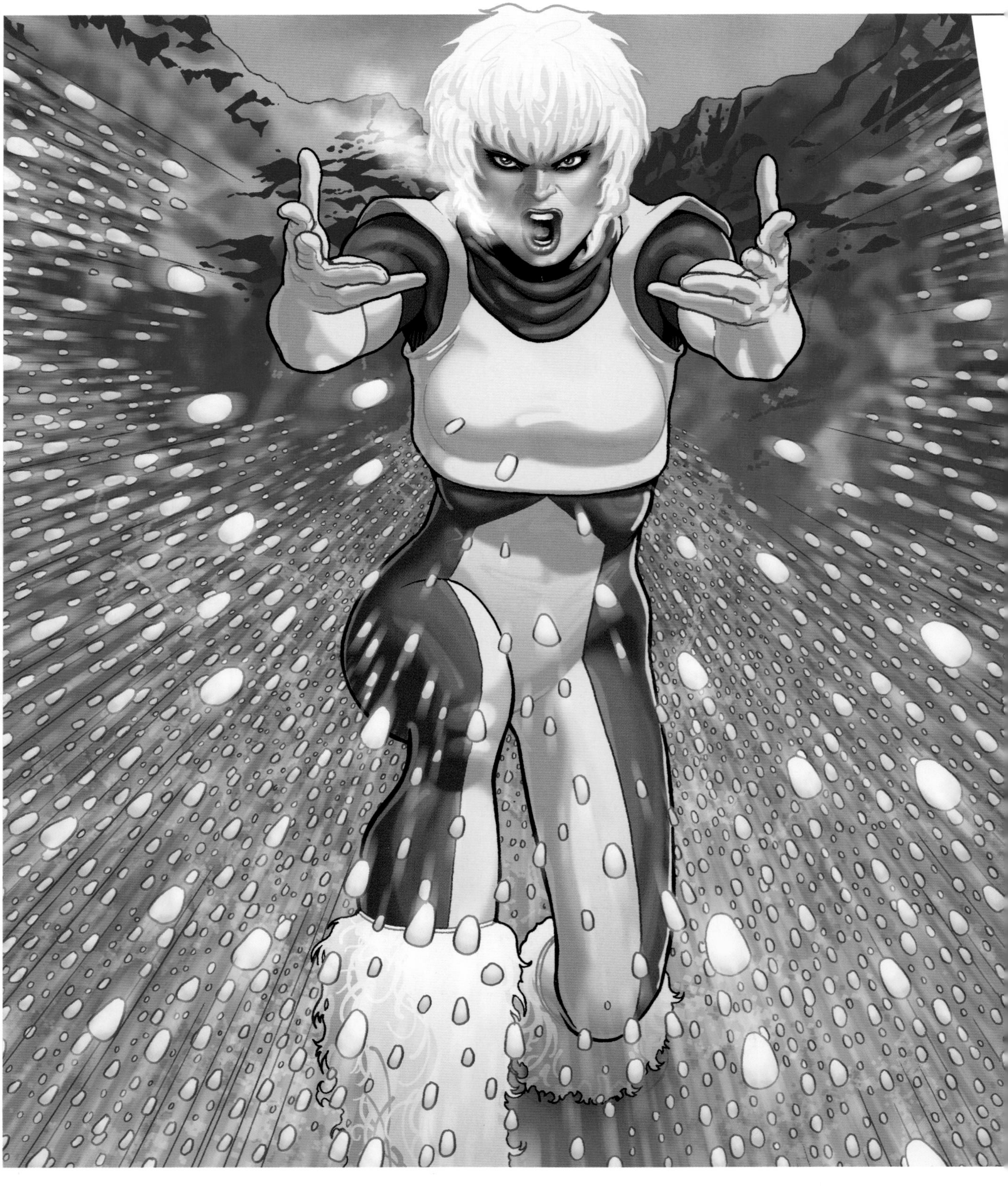

ICE

"One more **snow pun** and I will **never** speak to you **again.**"

Tora Olafsdotter was born with cryokinesis, the magical ability to generate and control ice. She can create deadly icicles, freeze enemies, and even manipulate the weather. As a child, Tora's Romani parents ran away with her from their Norwegian home. They were trying to protect Tora from bad people who wanted to use her powers to carry out evil deeds. Sadly, Tora accidentally killed her father while she was defending her family. To make sure her abilities would only be used to do good, Tora joined the Global Guardians team, an early version of the Justice League International (JLI).

Tora is honest, quiet, and always tries to see the best in people. Her best friend is her impulsive JLI teammate Beatriz da Costa. Beatriz is a Brazilian government agent who can generate green flames. Tora uses the Super Hero name Ice and Beatriz goes by Fire. Tora was briefly a member of the White Lantern Corps and has also assisted the Birds of Prey team. She and Fire still work together for the JLI.

DATA FILE

Friends and allies: Vixen (p14), Fire (p64)
Loves: Animals, cold weather
Enemies: Professor Ivo, the Black Lantern Corps

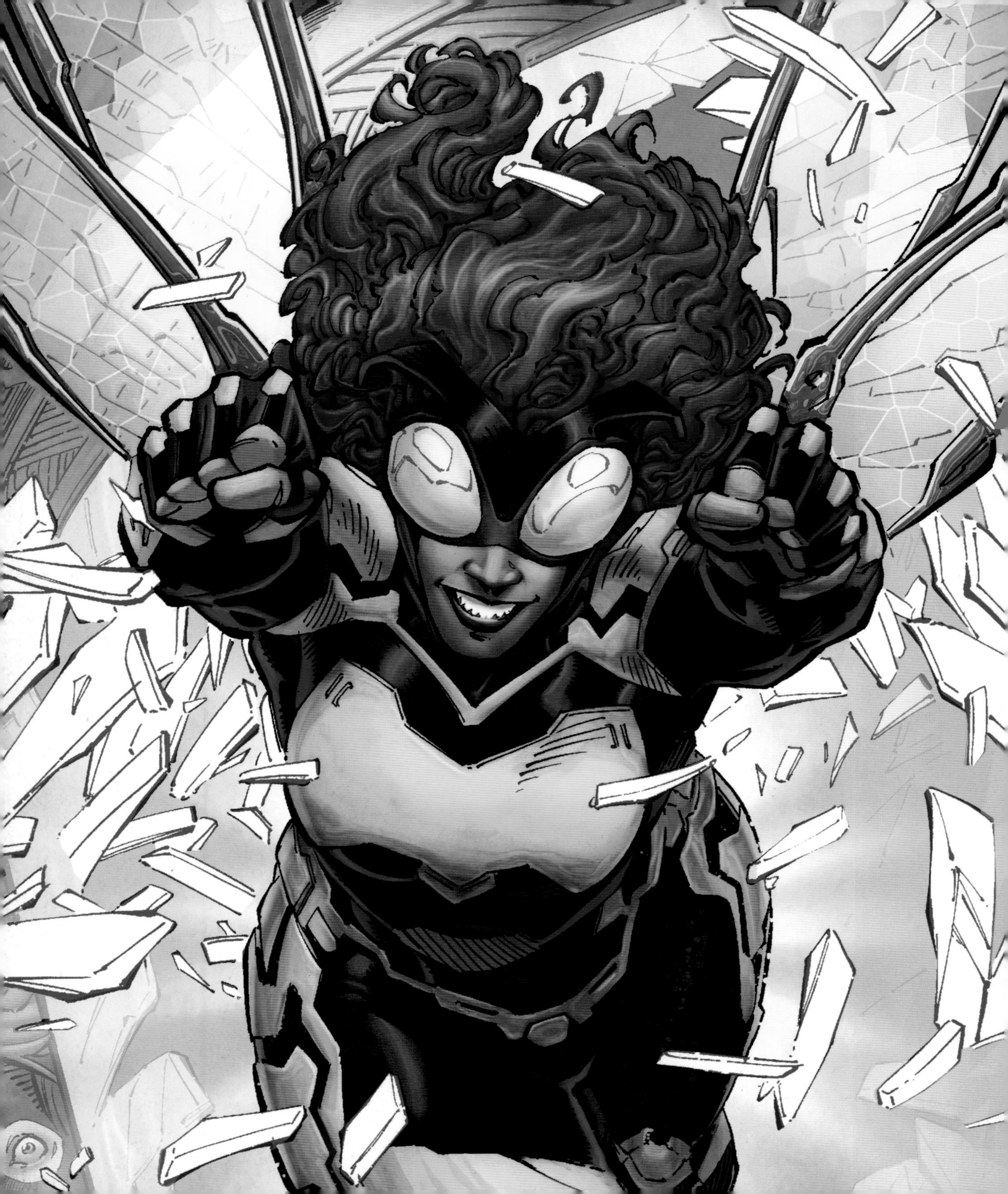

BOLD

These fearless Super Heroes are always first on the front line. Whether it is Lady Blackhawk taking down foes in her fighter jet, or Jesse Chambers speeding headfirst into danger, they are plucky, courageous, and daring heroes who will go to any lengths to fight the forces of evil. These brave women rush in where others fear to tread!

◄ **Bumblebee** (p36)

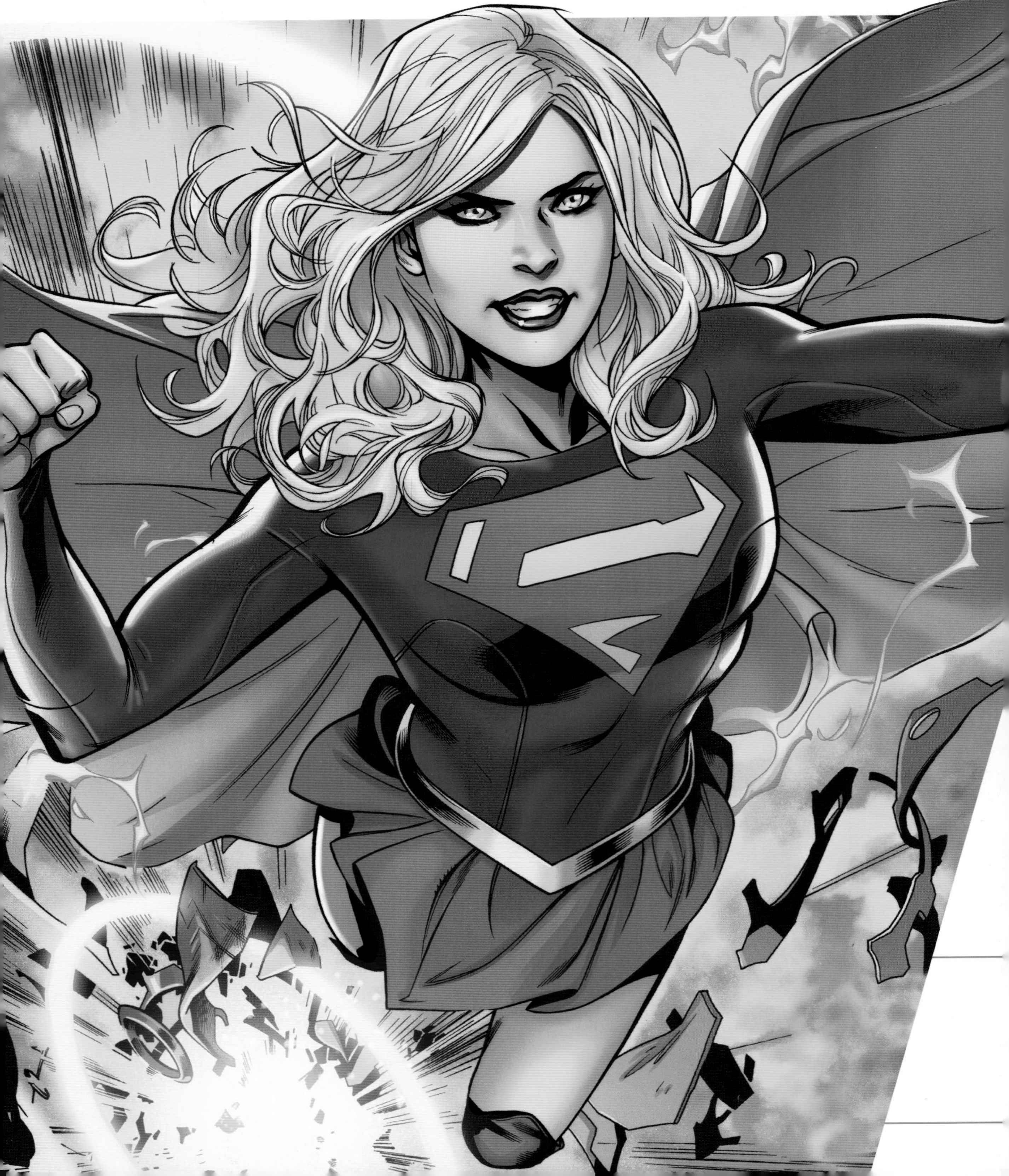

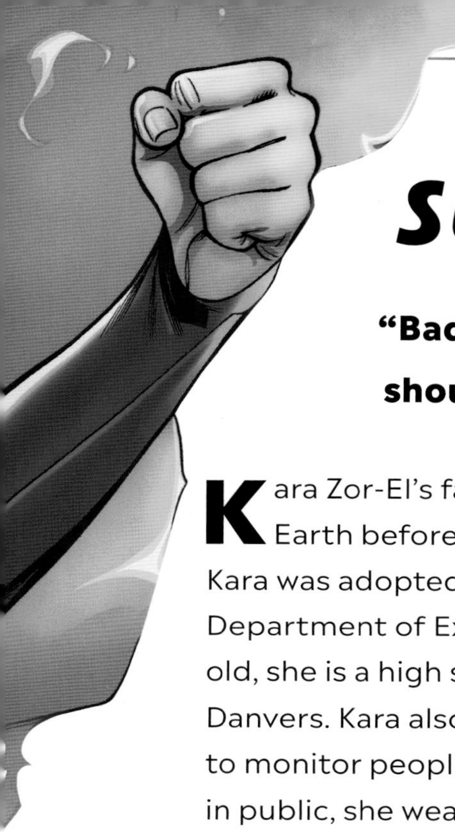

SUPERGIRL

"Bad dreams **don't** mean you should **stop dreaming.**"

Kara Zor-El's father placed her in a ship and sent her to Earth before her home planet, Krypton, was destroyed. Kara was adopted by the Danvers, two agents from the Department of Extranormal Operations (DEO). Now 16 years old, she is a high school student who goes by the name Kara Danvers. Kara also works alongside her parents at the DEO to monitor people with superpowers. To disguise her identity in public, she wears special glasses fitted with a holographic device that makes her hair appear brown to others.

Earth's yellow sun grants Kara the same powers as her cousin, Superman. She has super-strength, speed, vision, and hearing. She can fly, and is invulnerable to everything apart from magic and Kryptonite (a mineral from Krypton). While perfoming super heroics, Kara goes by the name Supergirl. Those who have seen her in action say that Kara—nicknamed the Girl of Steel—might even be more powerful than Superman. Kara is dedicated to fighting for justice, and believes this means trying to help villains as often as it means causing them harm.

DATA FILE

Friends and allies: Lois Lane (p74), Power Girl—Kara Zor-L (p114)
Occupation: Intern at CatCo Worldwide Media
Base: National City, CA

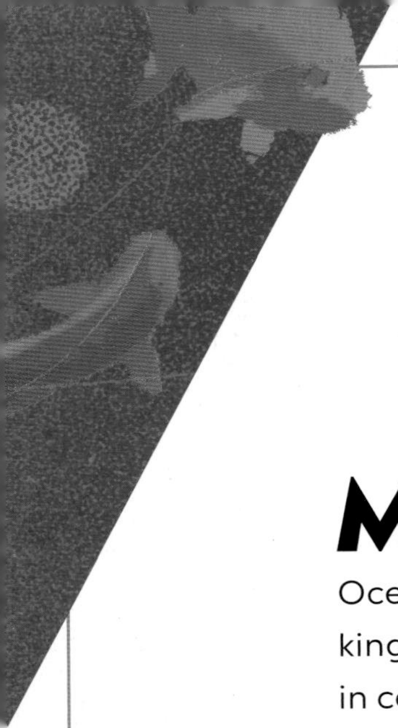

MERA

"I don't bow to any king."

Mera is the Queen of Atlantis, an advanced nation that lies deep under the water of the North Atlantic Ocean. She was born the princess of a rival underwater kingdom called Xebel. As Mera grew up, she was trained in combat and spying. When she was fully trained, her father commanded her to kill the king of Atlantis. Mera was shocked to discover that this king—Aquaman—was actually a kind and worthy ruler. Mera abandoned her father's plan. Instead, she followed the advice that her mother once gave her: to choose her own path in life.

Now, Mera rules over Atlantis alongside Aquaman with a strong but compassionate hand (and trident). Like all Xebellians, she adores being in the deep ocean. She is able to see in the dark and breathe underwater with ease. Mera also knows the royal Xebellian secret of hydrokinesis. This power allows her to control the water around her with her mind, willing it into any shape she chooses. Aquaman and Mera own a dog named Aquadog who unfortunately does not know how to swim.

DATA FILE

Friends and allies: Wonder Woman (p12), Hawkgirl (p76)

Occupations: Queen, diplomat

Base: Amnesty Bay, Atlantis

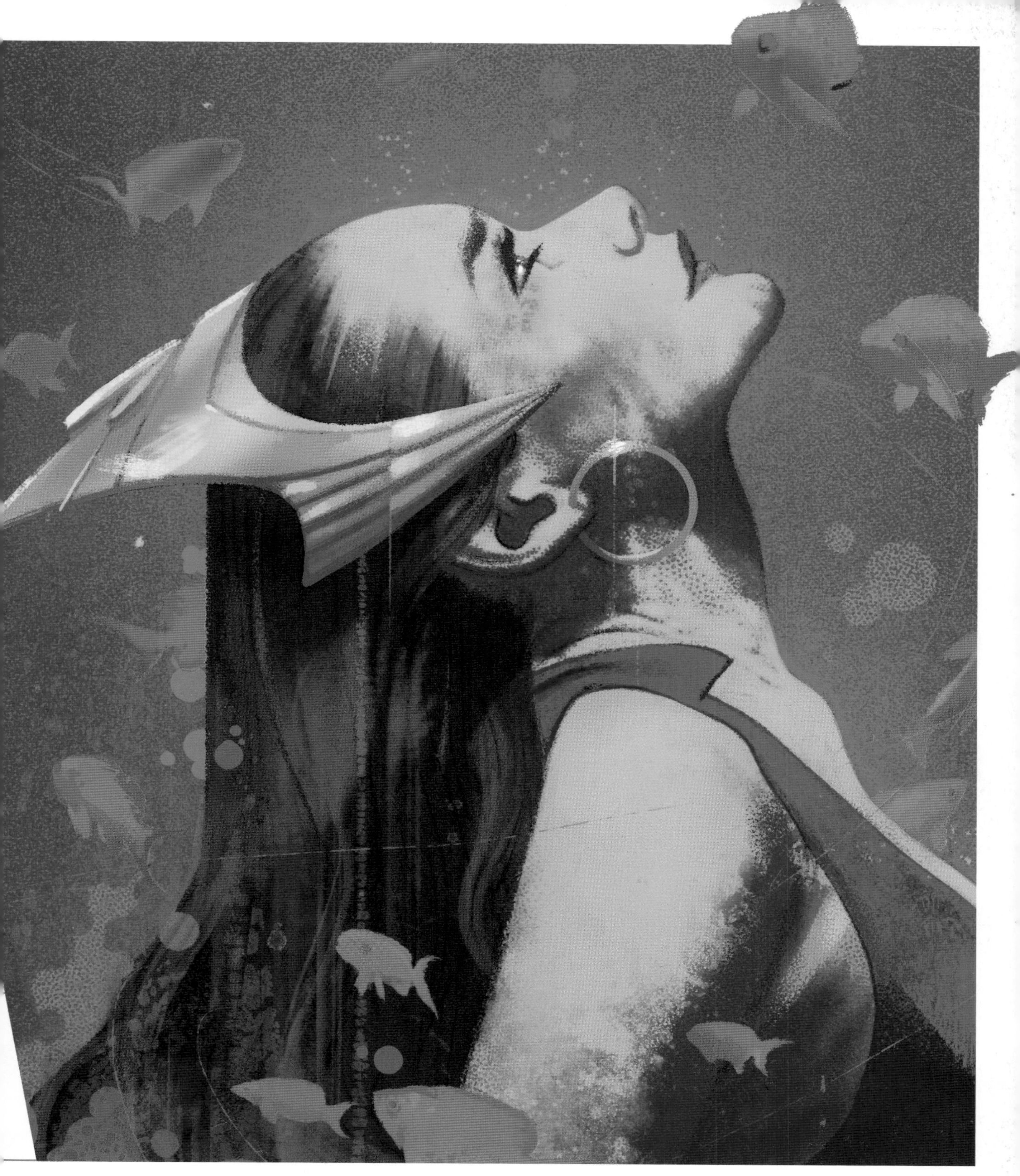

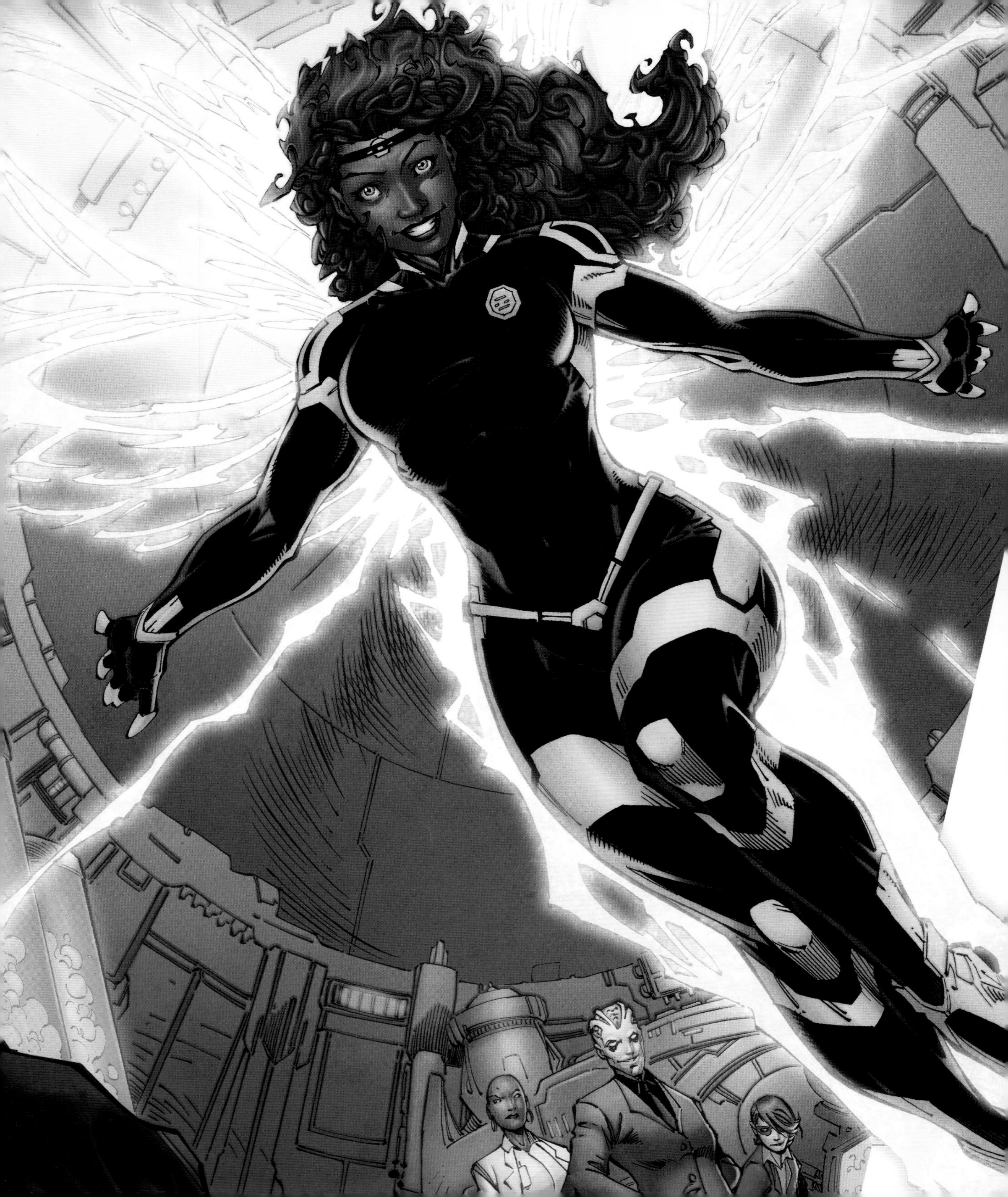

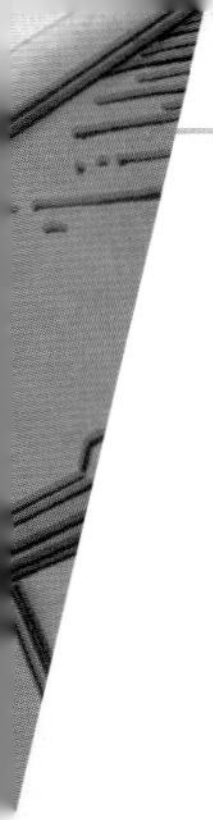

BUMBLEBEE

"I'm going to sting him back into the Stone Age!"

Karen Beecher is a strong-willed scientist and a member of the Teen Titans. Brave Karen goes by the Super Hero name Bumblebee. She built her own black-and-yellow super-suit, designed to protect her from enemy attacks. It also protects her from the rapid movement of her suit's wings as she flies through the air. Karen can shoot fire from her hands and shrink to tiny sizes. The lenses on her helmet are equipped with crystals that shoot electrical stings.

Karen met her boyfriend, the Teen Titan Mal Duncan, in a science laboratory. She originally designed the Bumblebee suit so she could pretend to fight Mal in front of the rest of his team and make him look impressive. Instead, the Titans found *her* so impressive they offered her a position on the squad. Karen has also worked as a weapons engineer for S.T.A.R. (Scientific and Technological Advanced Research) Labs. She and Mal have a young daughter. Karen has stepped back from her official Super Hero duties to focus on her family.

DATA FILE

Friends and allies: Donna Troy (p62), Elasti-Woman (p108)

Special skills: Positivity, invention

Base: San Francisco, CA

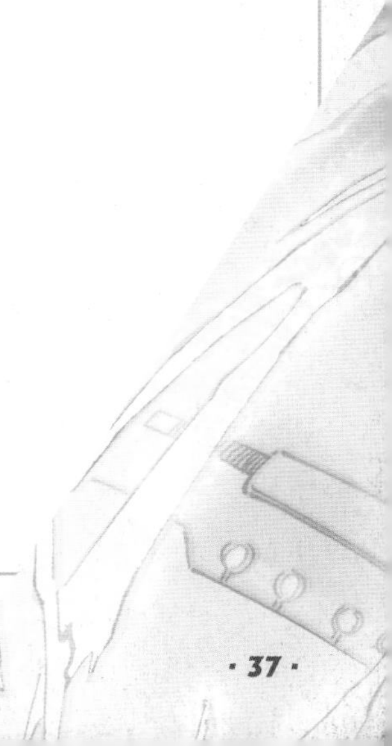

ETTA CANDY

"Who's ready to dance?"

Etta Candy is Wonder Woman's best friend. She is one of the first people Wonder Woman met after arriving in the mortal world. The two became close friends and teammates. Etta worked in the US Air Force before she joined A.R.G.U.S. (the Advanced Research Group Uniting Superhumans). This secret government agency was created after the formation of the Justice League. The agency cleans up the mess left behind by Super Heroes and villains during their mighty, supernatural fights.

Etta works closely with A.R.G.U.S.'s leader, Steve Trevor—the same man Wonder Woman rescued from the shores of Themyscira. Etta is skilled in battle strategy, combat, and the use of weapons. She has recently been promoted to the rank of Commander. Etta was once in love with archaeologist Dr. Barbara Minerva, but tragically Etta did not know Barbara's secret identity was the villain The Cheetah, Wonder Woman's worst enemy. Whenever she gets excited, Etta likes to shout "Woo woo!" She loves the television show *Friends*, and is a big fan of chocolate.

DATA FILE

Friend and ally: Wonder Woman (p12)
Base: Washington, D.C.
Loves: Protecting her friends

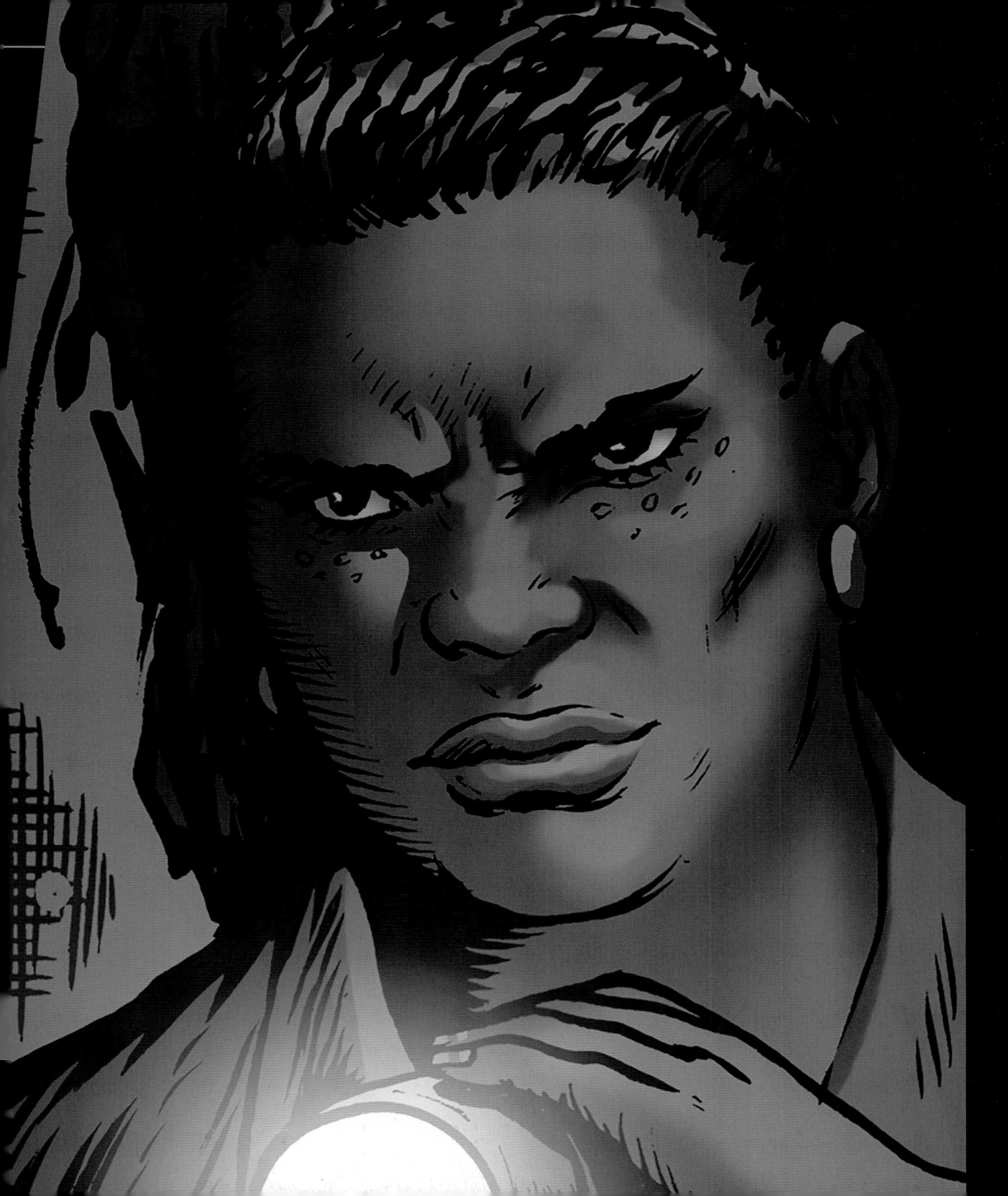

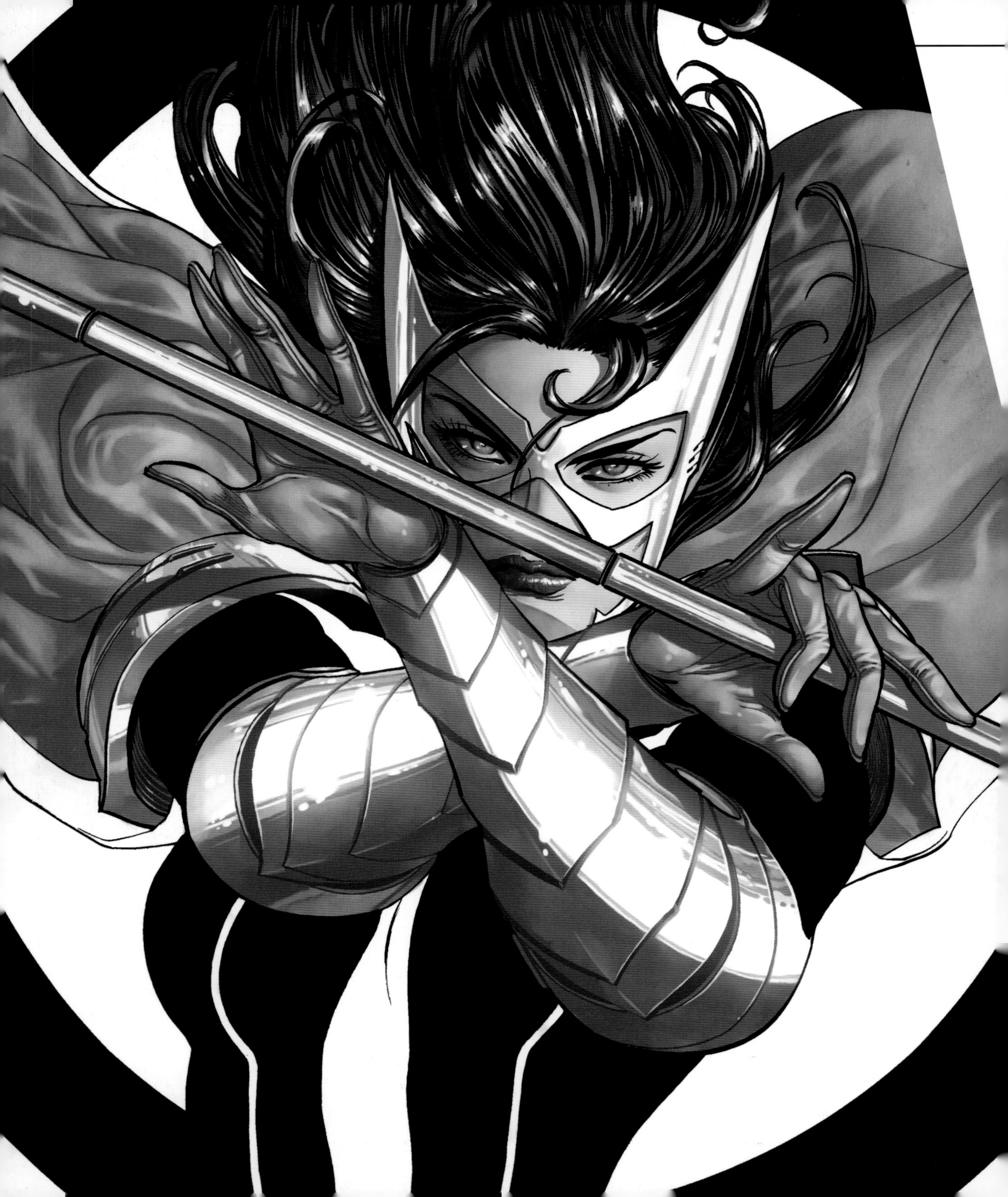

HUNTRESS

"I didn't come all this way **to be ignored. Respected,** certainly... **Yielded to,** definitely... But **never** ignored."

Helena Bertinelli ran away after the mysterious deaths of her parents, rather than take over the family business. Her father was a boss in the Sicilian Mafia, a dangerous criminal group. Instead, Helena became a member of a secret United Nations organization named Spyral. She partnered with teammate Dick Grayson (once known as the Super Hero Nightwing) to hunt down valuable historical artifacts. Helena eventually left Spyral and dedicated her life to toppling the criminal group that included members of her own family.

Unstoppable with a crossbow in her hand, Helena is now the crime fighter best known as Huntress. She is part of the Birds of Prey team, working with Batgirl (Barbara Gordon) and Black Canary (Dinah Drake) in Gotham City. She helps Barbara and Dinah keep the city's streets safe from the forces of evil. Helena works as a teacher when she is not practicing her archery. She is famous for her pointed mask and sharp wit.

DATA FILE

Friends and allies: Black Canary (p16), Power Girl—Tanya Spears (p78)
Special skill: Fluent in Italian
Base: Gotham City

LIGHTNING

"No offense... but I'm like a billion orders of magnitude more powerful than you."

Jennifer Pierce inherited her superpowers from her father Jefferson, better known as the Super Hero Black Lightning. Jennifer is able to transform her entire body into lightning. This allows her to fly and to project energy outward in blasts. She also absorbs any electricity with which she comes into contact. This makes it impossible for her to use any objects powered by electricity, including cell phones and televisions.

Jefferson insisted that both his daughters finish their education before they became crime fighters. Unlike her older sister Anissa, strong-willed Jennifer ignored her father's wishes and began defending the innocent when she was still a teenager. Jefferson eventually came to respect confident Jennifer's choices. He found her a place with the Justice Society of America team. She fights under the name Lightning, a complement to Anissa's Super Hero name Thunder. Jennifer briefly teamed up with Batgirl, Stargirl, and Supergirl under Wonder Woman's leadership to protect Washington, D.C., from aliens.

DATA FILE

Friends and allies: Stargirl (p48), Thunder (p86)
Base: Chicago, IL
Special skill: Flying at light speed

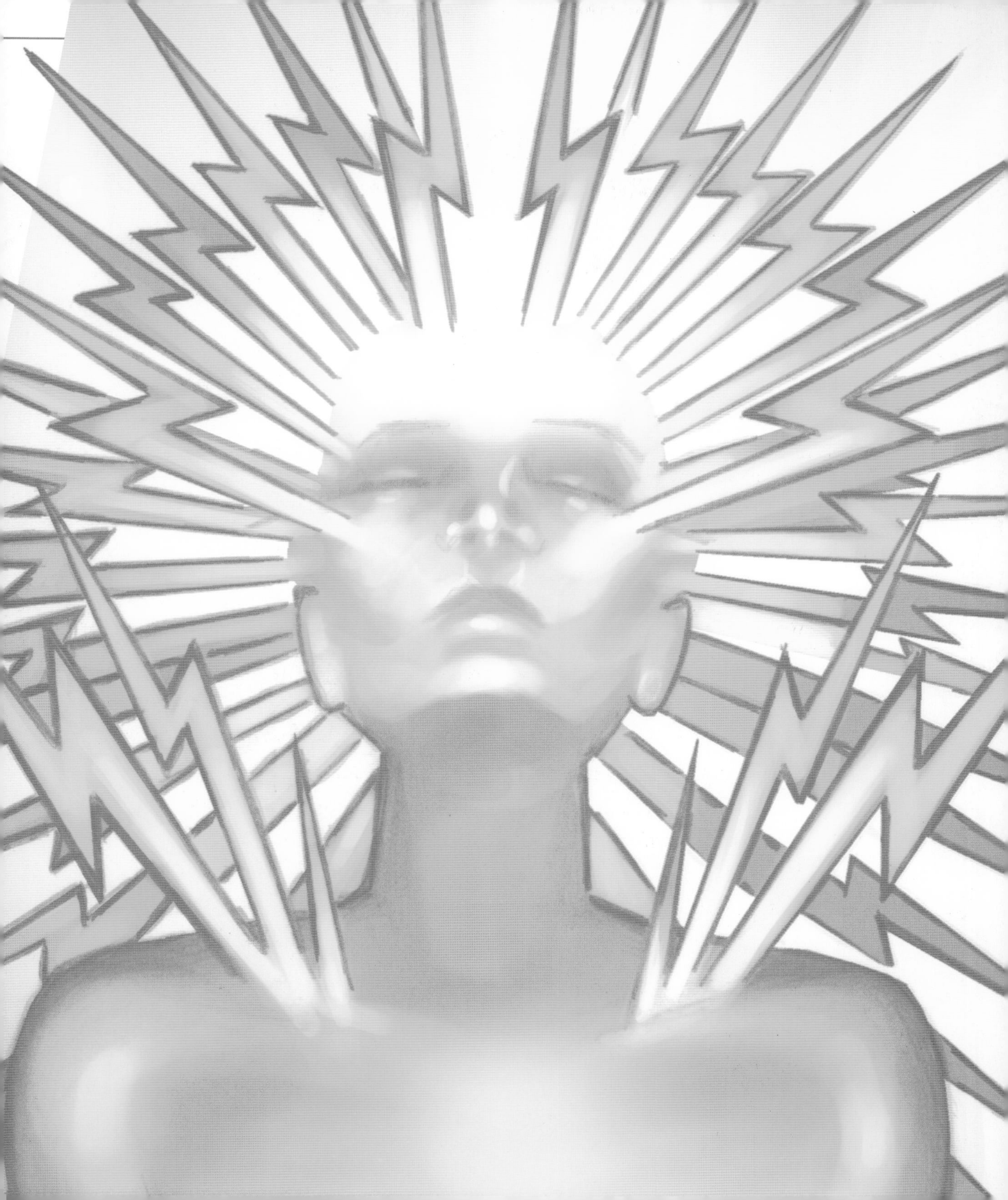

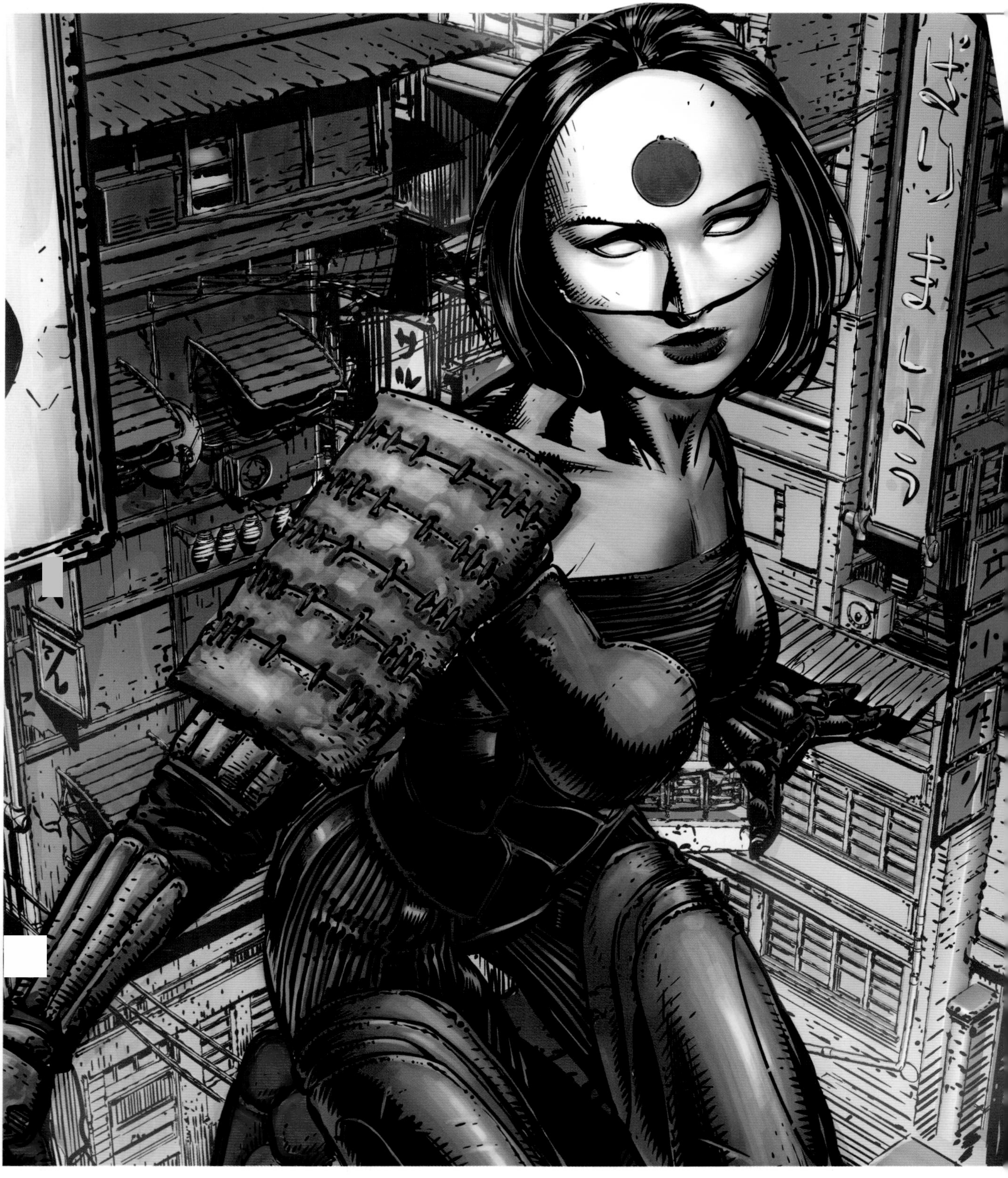

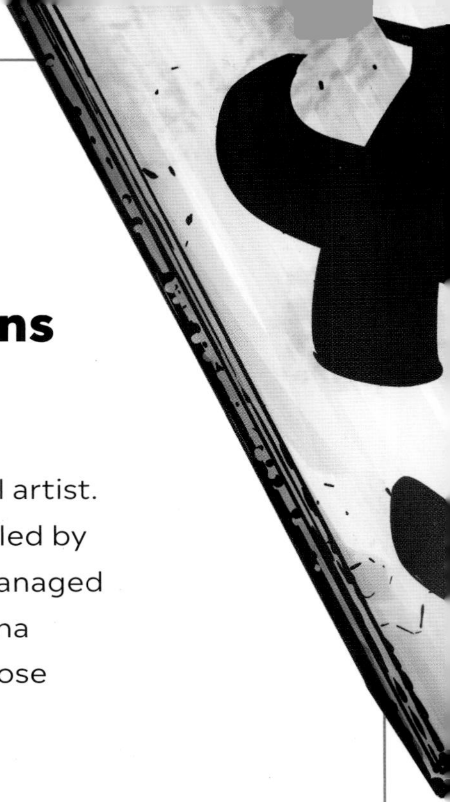

KATANA

"You and your **cowardly minions** had better start **running.**"

Yamashiro Tatsu was a Japanese Olympic martial artist. She lost her family when they were tragically killed by a jealous member of the Yakuza crime gang. Tatsu managed to escape with a mystical sword, a 14th-century katana named Soultaker. The sword contains the souls of those it has killed, and chose Tatsu as its rightful owner. Tatsu dedicated herself to finding those responsible for the loss of her family, taking on the name Katana.

While searching for revenge, Katana began fighting to protect those in need as a member of The Outsiders. They are a group of superpowered outcasts and misfits. The Outsiders take on missions that other teams like the Justice League cannot, in case it harms their reputations. Dedicated and focused, Katana has also been a valuable member of the Birds of Prey group. Her sword can damage any enemy, no matter how powerful. Katana is certain that her husband's soul lives in her blade, and talks to him often.

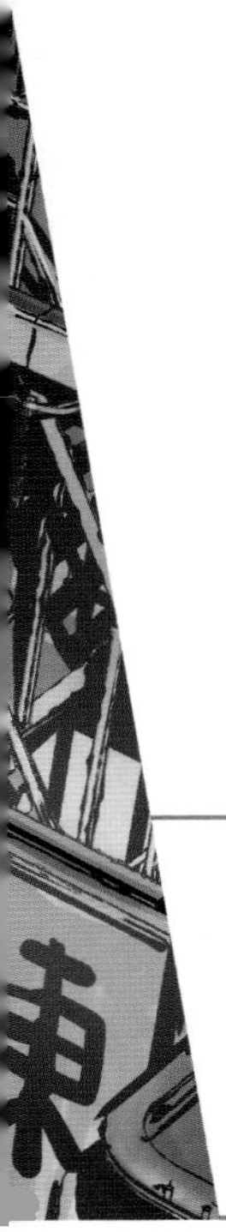

DATA FILE

Friends and allies: Frost (p80), Catwoman (p100)

Enemies: The Yakuza, Ra's al Ghul

Loves: Her sword, payback

LADY BLACKHAWK

"We need a name. This 'agents' thing—it's got no zing. So, what about being the Birds of Prey?"

Zinda Blake was the first woman to become a part of the Blackhawk Squadron—a band of skilled pilots who fought against the Nazis in World War II. The all-male team originally told Zinda that women could not be Blackhawks. However, they allowed her to join as an honorary member after she rescued their entire squad from an evil pirate named Scavenger. Zinda is an expert at combat both on the ground and in the air. She is as deadly with a gun in her hand as she is in the cockpit of her plane.

Zinda was thrown forward through time in a supernatural event, landing her in the present day. She took on the radio call sign "Lady Blackhawk" and teamed up with the Birds of Prey, becoming the group's pilot. She flies a jet named the *Aerie One*. Zinda briefly tried to become an actress, but discovered she is better suited to flying. She is able to order a drink in thirty different languages.

DATA FILE

Friends and allies: Big Barda (p50), Batgirl (p72)
Loves: Cooking, dancing
Special skill: Flying any aircraft

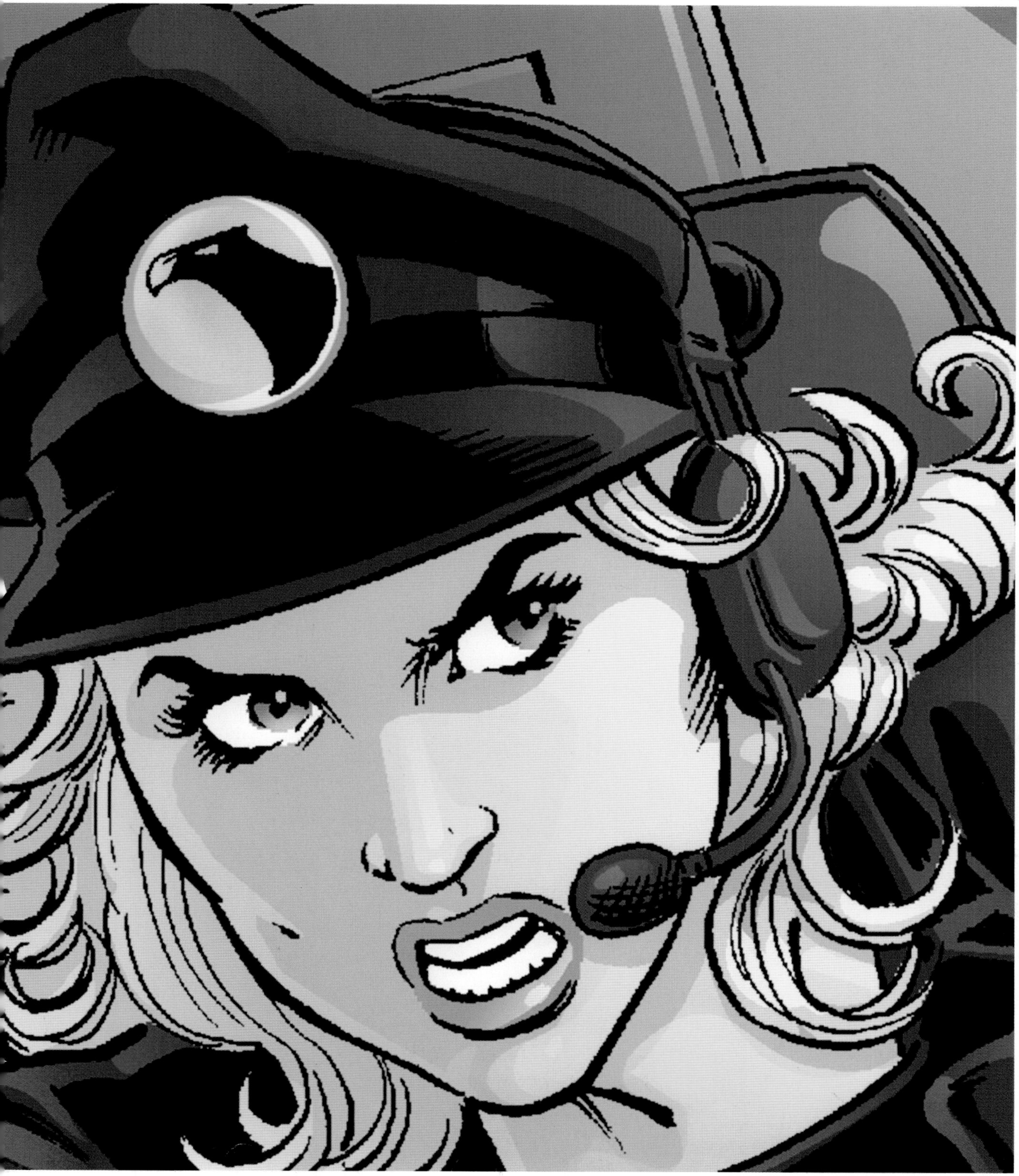

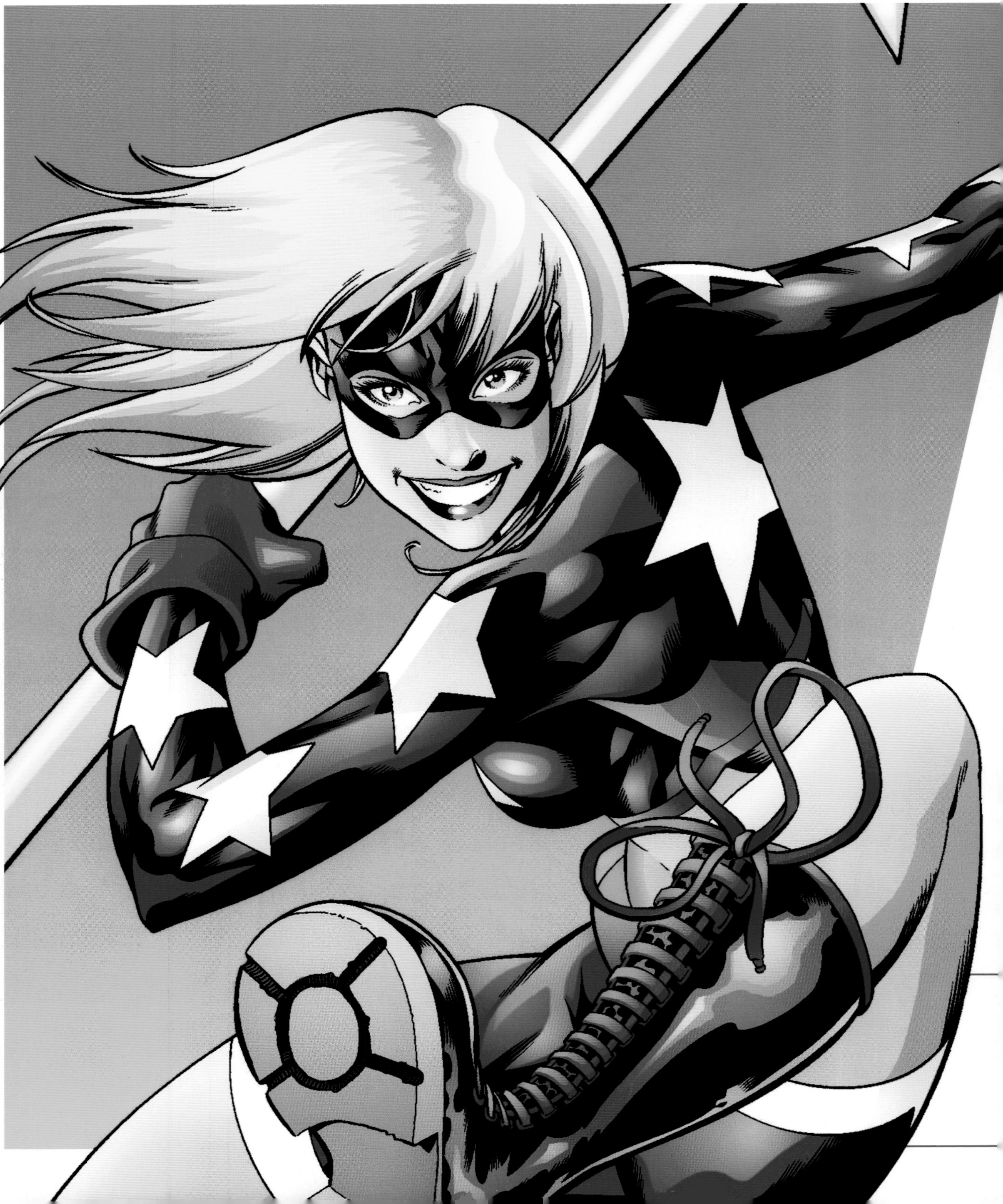

STARGIRL

"Nothing like **flying** on a sunny day."

Courtney Whitmore was devastated when her parents divorced. She was forced to move from Los Angeles to Nebraska, where her mother's new husband lived. Courtney struggled to make friends at her new high school. While cleaning out her stepfather's office, she discovered he had previously been the sidekick to a Super Hero, and had kept that hero's belongings. Courtney grabbed the Cosmic Converter Belt, the Cosmic Staff, and the star-covered shirt she found, and decided to become her own hero.

Going by the name Stargirl, Courtney was videotaped saving civilians from a fire and became a viral hit online. Her staff and belt harness the power of starlight, which allows her to fly, levitate objects, and manipulate energy. Courtney can create force fields or blast her foes with stellar power. Bubbly, intelligent, and kind, Courtney has been a member of and a spokesperson for the Justice League of America and Justice League United teams.

DATA FILE

Friends and allies: Wonder Woman (p12), Power Girl—Kara Zor-L (p114)
Loves: California, social media
Base: Los Angeles, CA

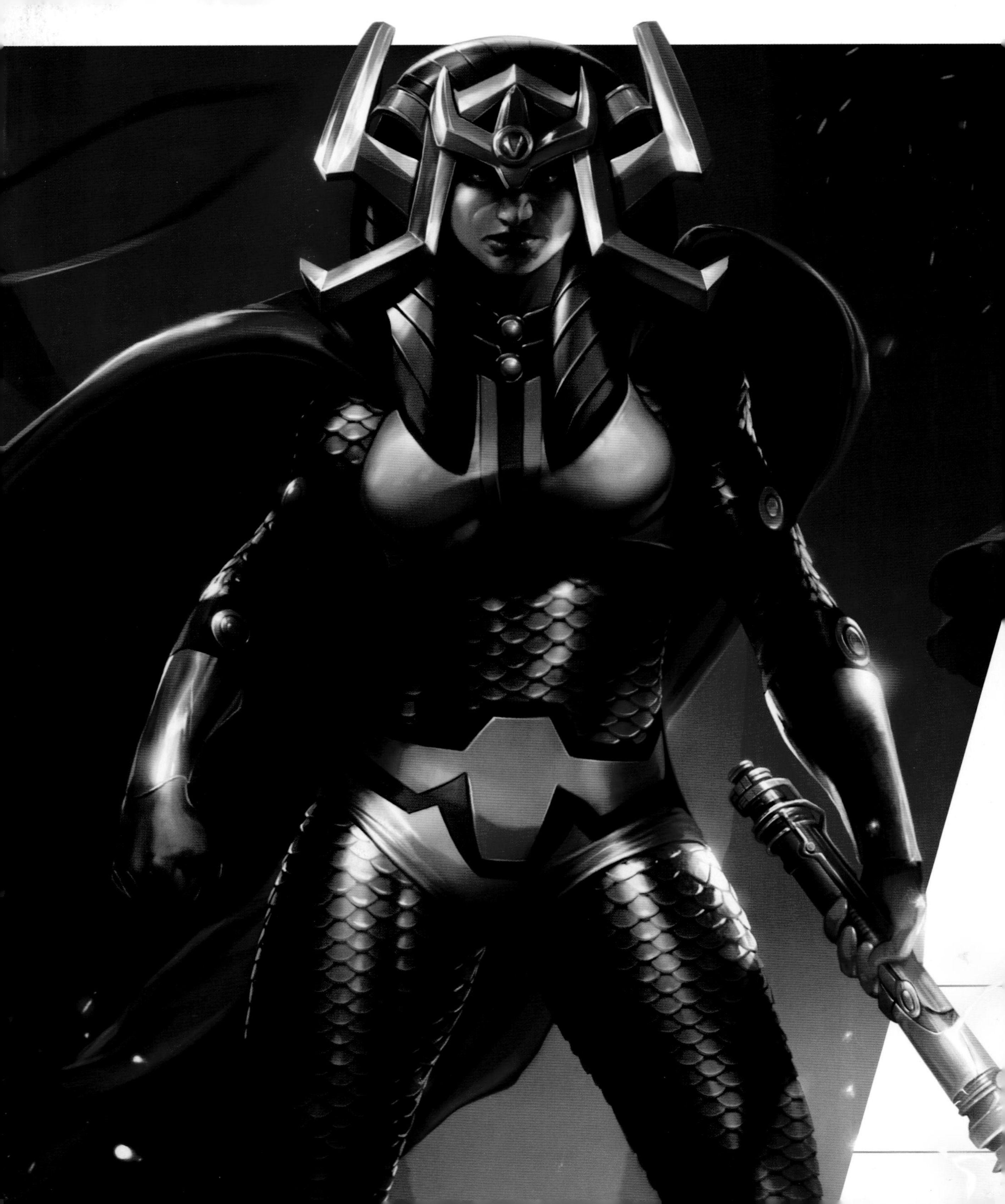

BIG BARDA

"Love... is being loved. Everyone needs love... especially the strong... especially those who fear it most!"

Big Barda is one of the New Gods, a race of aliens from the planet Apokolips with super-strength and immortality. She is extremely tall. Barda was trained from childhood in the art of battle by the forces of the brutal ruler Darkseid. She quickly became the strongest warrior on Apokolips, and the leader of the Female Furies battalion. Heroic Barda eventually recognized that Darkseid was evil and rebelled against her home planet, fleeing to Earth.

Soon after, Barda joined the Justice League team. She was also the strongest member of the Birds of Prey, and has even worked as a magician's assistant! She briefly ran a self-defense program for women called the New Female Furies in New York City. Barda's beloved weapon, the Mega-Rod, can create teleportation tunnels, increase the force of gravity, and release energy bolts. She is married to Darkseid's son, Scott Free (also known as Mister Miracle), and they have a son named Jacob.

DATA FILE

Friends and allies: Lady Blackhawk (p46), Batgirl (p72)
Special skills: Intimidation, combat
Loves: Intimidation, combat

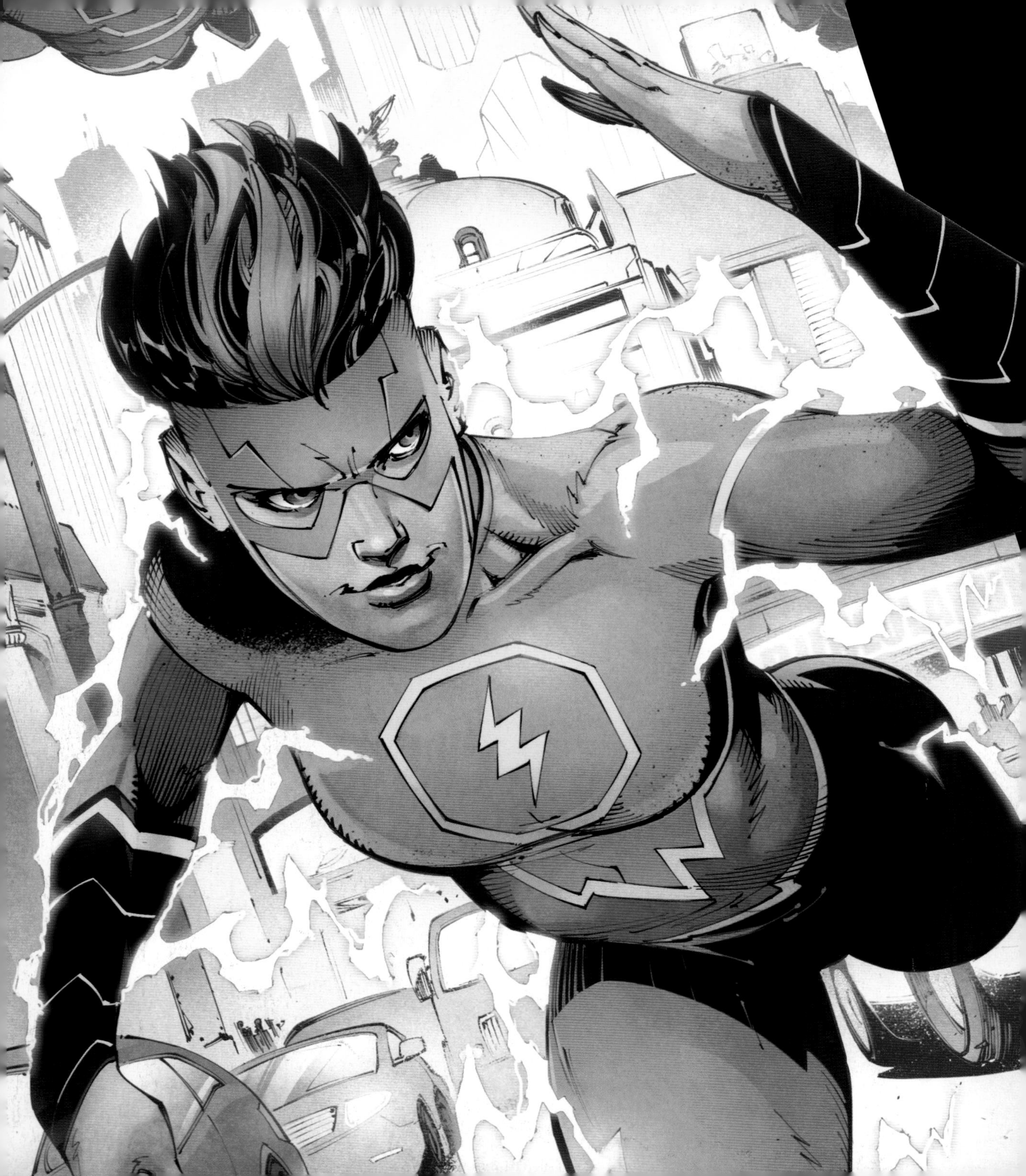

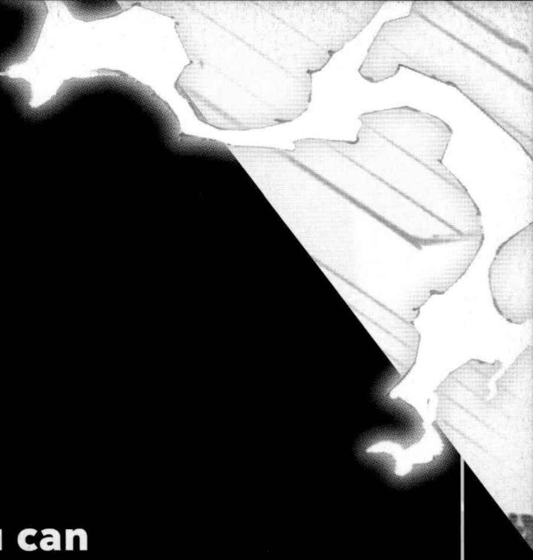

THE FLASH OF CHINA

"All I do is run. You really think you can beat me at my one thing?"

Avery Ho is a Chinese-American teenager who got caught in a Speed Force Storm in Central City. Avery was struck by the intense energy of the Storm—a cosmic force responsible for moving time forward. She gained the same powers as heroic speedster The Flash, including super-speed and durability. Avery learned to control her new abilities at the Speed Force Academy, run by scientist Meena Dhawan.

Avery moved overseas to join the Justice League of China. She can vibrate her body super-fast to phase through solid objects, turn invisible, and shoot cyclones from her hands. Avery's punch is so powerful that she has even pushed the mighty New Super-Man backward. Edgy and energetic, Avery sometimes finds it difficult to balance being both a "normal" teenage girl and a Super Hero. Avery's suit and hair are a cool combination of purple, black, and gold.

DATA FILE

Friends and allies: Jesse Chambers (p56), Iris West (p120)

Special skills: Fluent in English and Mandarin

Base: Jilin Province, China

LANA LANG

"Let's try **not** to **make friends** with any more **monsters.**"

Lana Lang grew up with her best friend Clark Kent in their small Kansas town. Always smart and studious, Lana left Clark and Smallville behind after high school to find her own way in the world. Now, Lana works as an electrical engineer abroad. She is also a part-time journalist for the *Daily Planet* newspaper, writing articles on advanced science.

Lana and Clark remain friends. She has always known and kept his secret identity of Superman. In fact, when Superman needs help to save the world, Lana will often provide him with expert engineering advice. She even took on the name Superwoman for a time. After absorbing radioactive energy from Superman's body, Lana gained superpowers and wore Kryptonian Battle Armor to fight the forces of evil. She had to surrender her powers to protect herself and the city of Metropolis, but Lana is still a brave and daring hero. Lana is engaged to John Henry Irons, the uncle of young Super Hero Natasha Irons (Steel). Natasha and Lana are very close friends.

DATA FILE

Friends and allies: Lois Lane (p74), Steel (p84)
Place of birth: Smallville, KS
Enemies: M1dn1ght, Lena Luthor

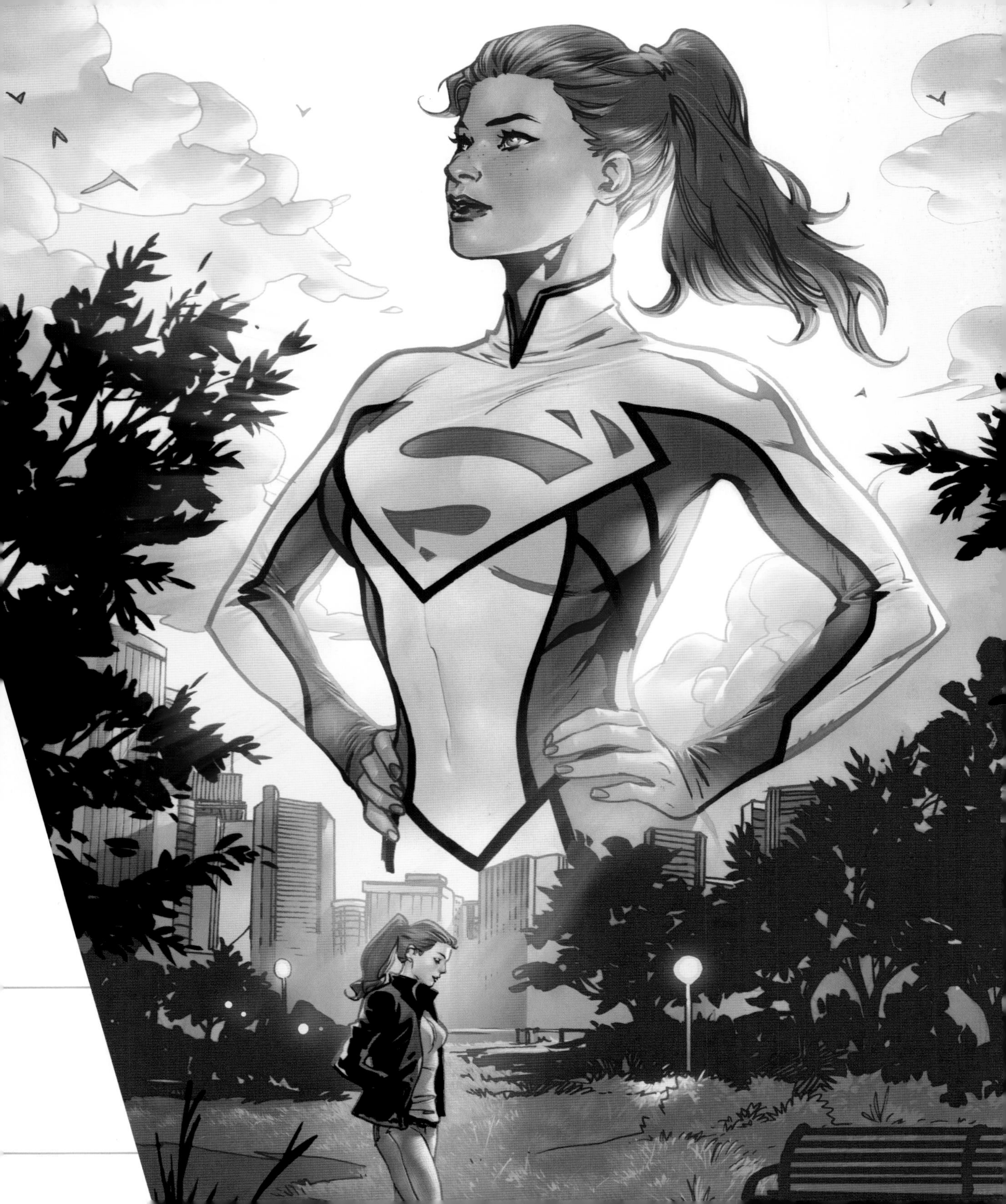

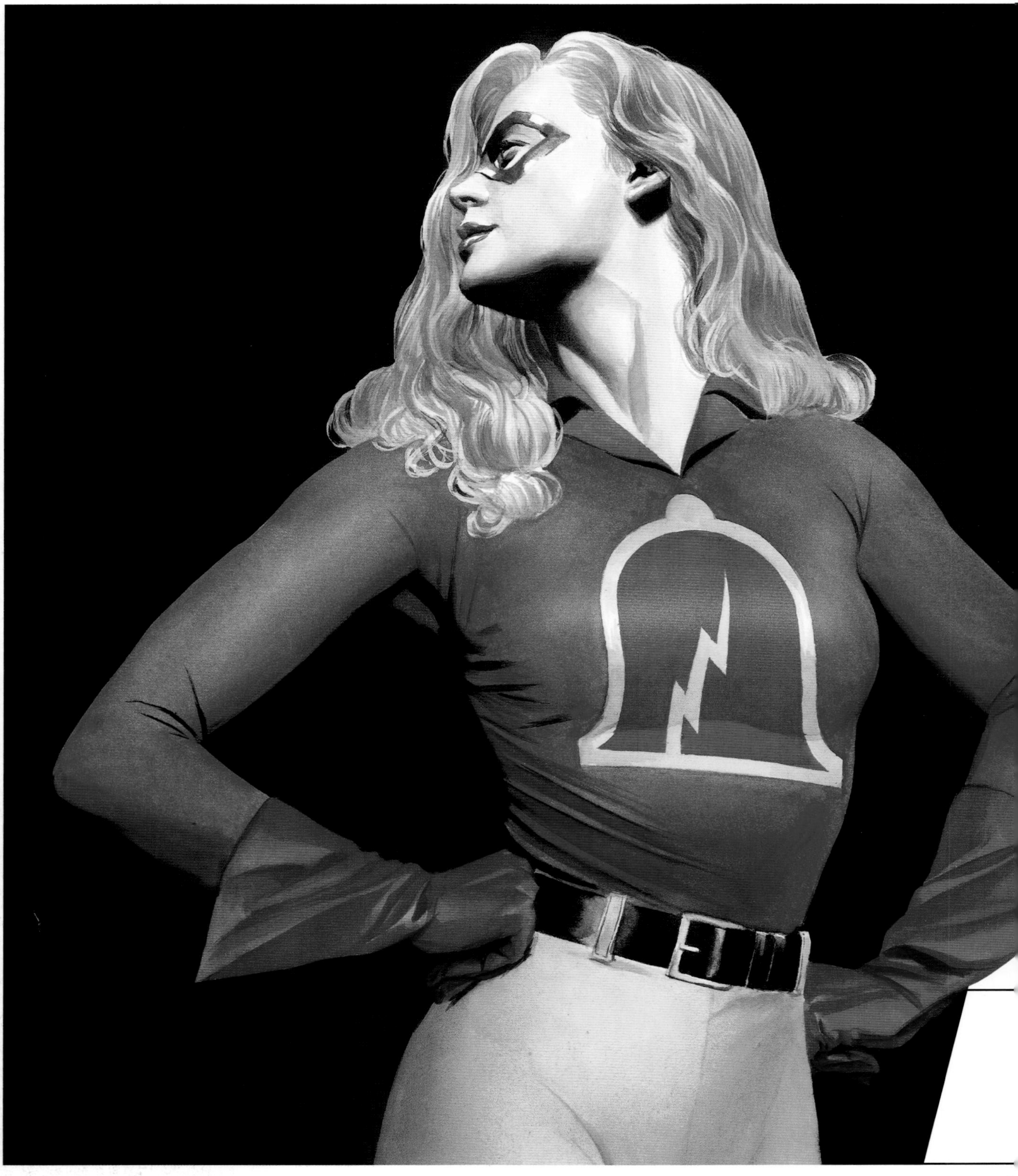

JESSE CHAMBERS

"Now—are you going to **cooperate,** or do I have to get **angry?!**"

Jesse Chambers is the daughter of two Super Heroes, Johnny Quick and Liberty Belle, from whom she inherited her amazing powers. From her mother, Jesse gained super-strength, reflexes, and stamina. From her father, Jesse learned a magical mathematical formula—and when she says it out loud, she gains super-speed and flight! For her Super Hero name, Jesse once went by Jesse Quick (in honor of her dad), but she now uses her mom's former title, Liberty Belle.

Jesse attended Gotham University before she took over her family's broadcast media company, Quickstart Enterprises. Like her father, Jesse is an honorary member of the Justice Society of America, of which she was also business manager. Jesse has worked alongside many other heroes with speedster powers and is eager to continue her family's legacy. Between her office job and her work as a Super Hero, Jesse is a determined leader and workaholic—but she loves what she does.

DATA FILE

Friends and allies: The Flash of China (p52), Iris West (p120)
Enemies: Reverse-Flash, Damage
Place of birth: Queens, NY

RENEE MONTOYA

"It's an **interesting** question..."

Renee Montoya is an officer for the Gotham City Police Department (GCPD). The daughter of Dominican immigrants, she graduated top of her class from Police Academy and took a job in the Major Crimes division. She secretly began training with The Question, a masked journalist who left behind a card with a question mark wherever he investigated. After The Question was killed, Renee put on his mask and continued his work.

Renee's mask is made of a special material called "Pseudoderm" that perfectly imitates skin and makes her face look completely blank. In addition to her GCPD studies in crime, weapons, and investigation, Renee has an unusual talent. Thanks to her training with The Question, she has learned how to control her nervous system—she can stop herself from feeling pain or fear. Tough and reserved, Renee is fully dedicated to finding the truth. Anyone with an unsolved crime who needs The Question's investigative skills can contact Renee on her website. She is sometimes in a relationship with Kate Kane, better known as Batwoman.

DATA FILE

Friends and allies: Batgirl (p72), Batwoman (p96)
Enemies: Two-Face, the Crime Syndicate
Base: Gotham City

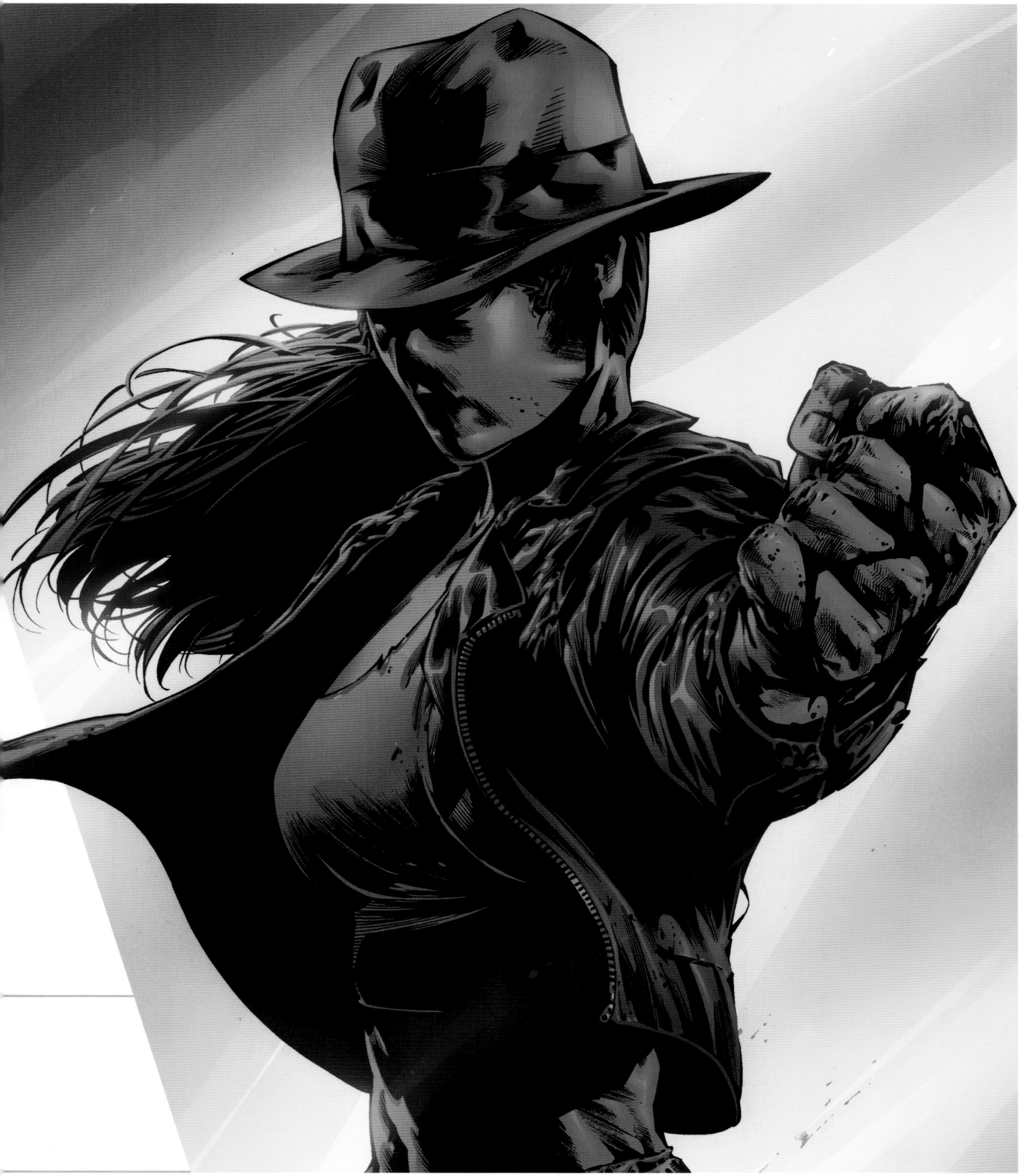

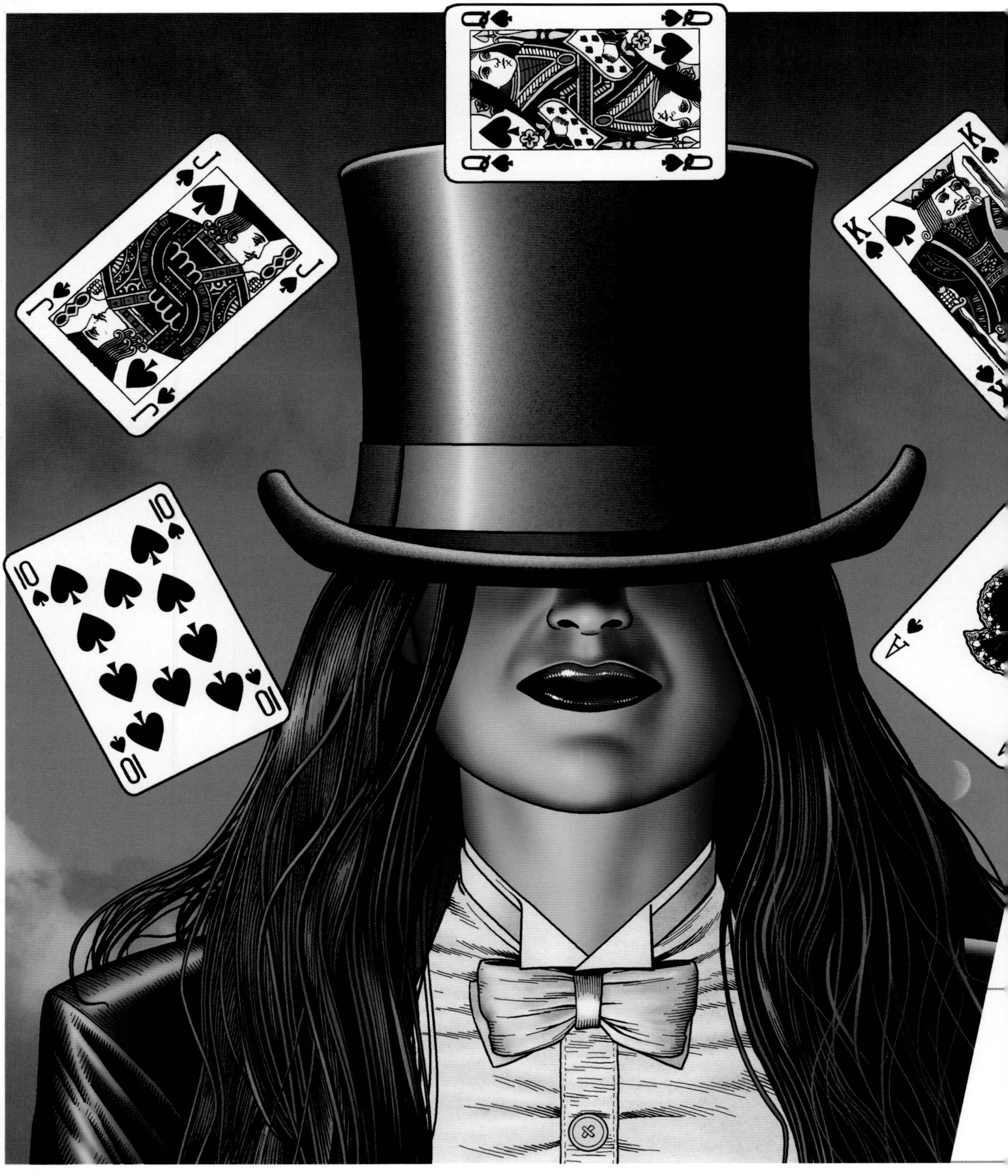

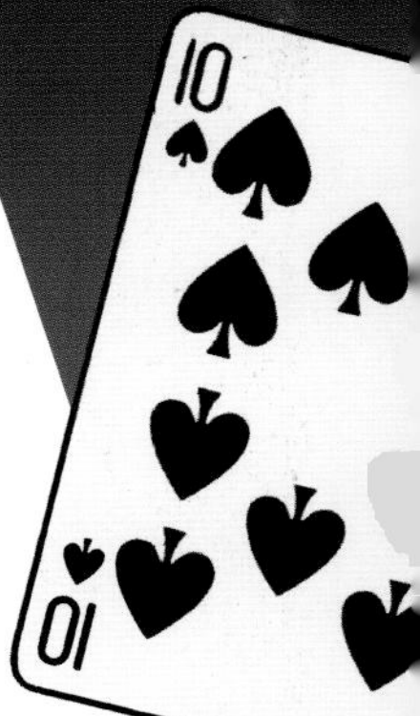

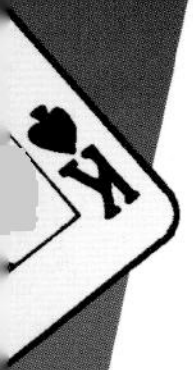

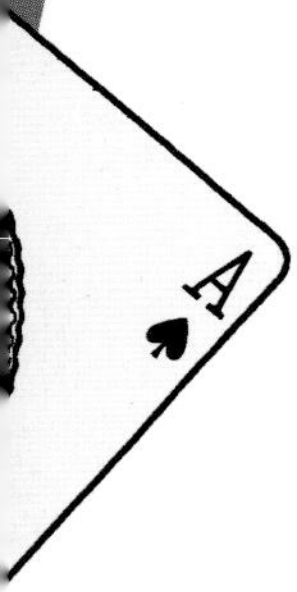

ZATANNA

"I'm a spellaholic."

Zatanna Zatara is both a stage magician and one of the world's most powerful sorcerers. Following in her father's footsteps as an illusionist, she performs incredible escapes and other tricks. Zatanna discovered the magic within her was actually real while she was investigating her father's disappearance. She casts spells by speaking them backward—for example, "leaH em!" will heal her, as it is "Heal me!" spoken in reverse. Anything that stops her from speaking puts Zatanna in serious danger.

Now nearly unmatched in sorcery, Zatanna can also control the weather, objects, peoples' will, gravity, energy, time, and space. She is so quick with her hands while performing card tricks that almost no one can figure out how she does her "Zatara shuffle." She has helped to defend Gotham City from vampires and is a member of the magical Justice League Dark team. Zatanna famously wears a black-and-white tuxedo, complete with a bow tie and a top hat.

DATA FILE

Friends and allies: Wonder Woman (p12), Amethyst (p18)

Special skills: Lockpicking, pulling small animals from hats

Base: Washington, D.C.

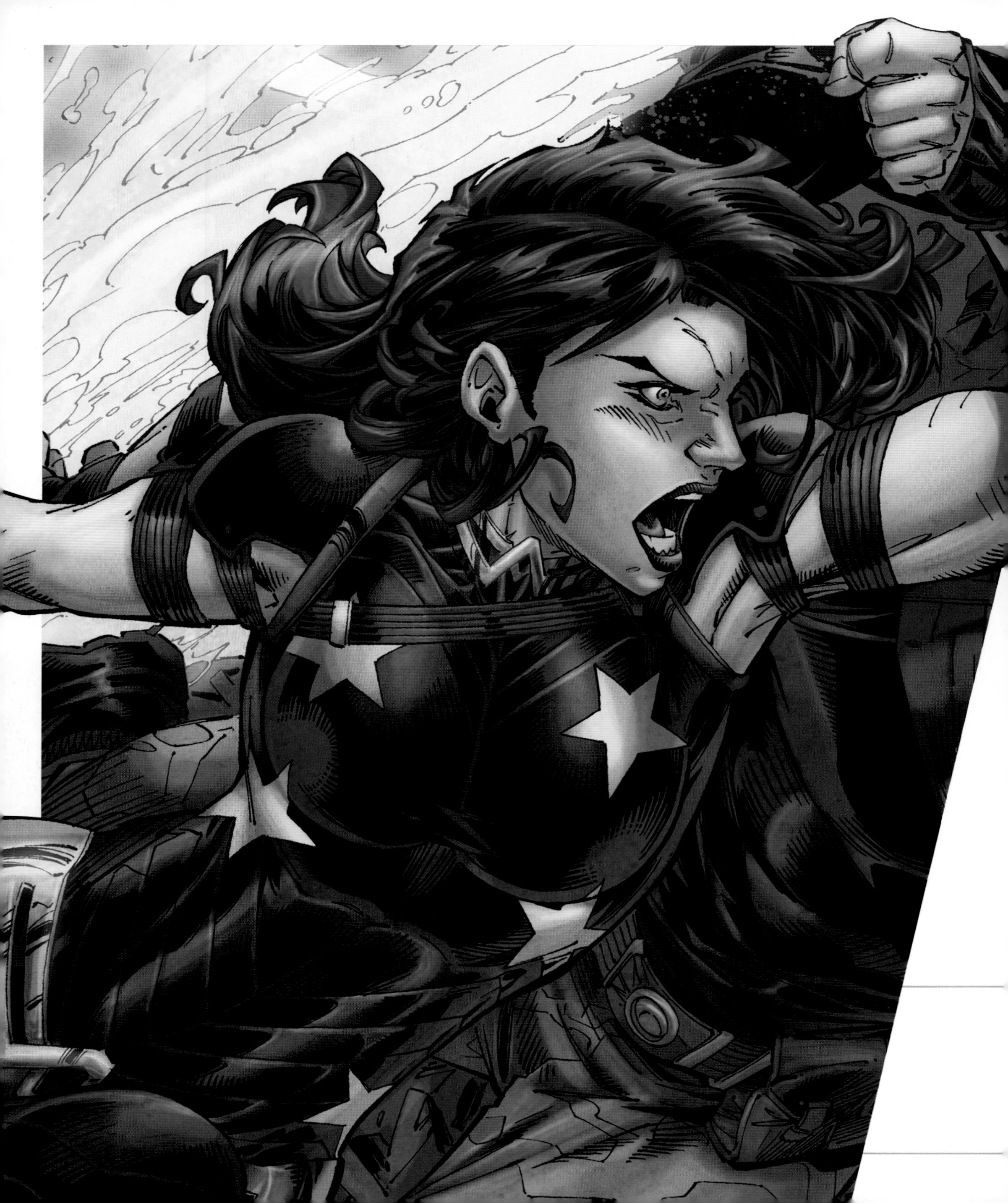

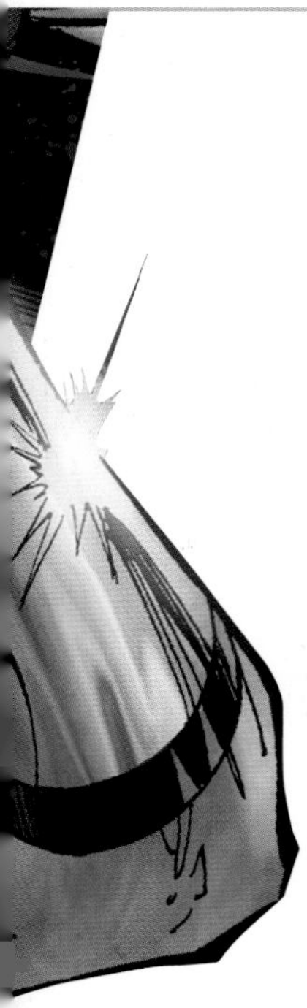

DONNA TROY

"Titans would be the first ones in. No hesitation. Kids have no fear."

Donna Troy was created from clay by an evil sorceress as part of a plan to claim Wonder Woman's crown. The plan failed and Donna was rescued by the same Amazons she was sent to destroy. They magically replaced her childhood memories, convincing Donna that Wonder Woman raised her on Themyscira. Trained as an Amazon, Donna is nearly equal in strength and power to Wonder Woman herself, and wears her own pair of bulletproof gauntlets. She is able to perfectly imitate the voice of anyone she hears.

After traveling to the mortal world, Donna joined forces with the Teen Titans group as the Super Hero Wonder Girl. Loyal and courageous, she is the Titans' current leader, helping to defeat many threats to the universe. Donna struggles with angry feelings due to her confusion over her childhood, but she is learning how to manage them. She owns a black Pegasus named Discordia, who can instantly transport her across long distances.

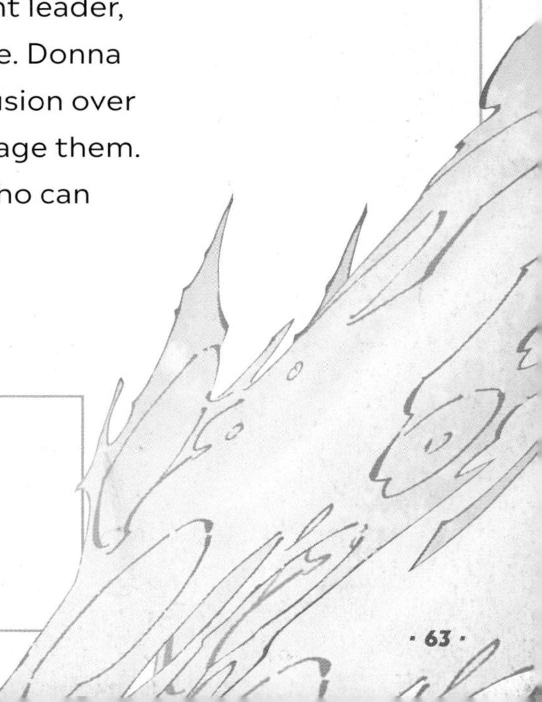

DATA FILE

Friends and allies: Miss Martian (p22), Bumblebee (p36)

Special skills: Photography, fencing

Loves: Her Titans family, justice

FIRE

"I was a spy for years... Believe me, I know more about investigation than the two of you put together."

Beatriz Bonilla da Costa sometimes goes by the nicknames Bea or B.B., but is best known as the Super Hero Fire. A former model, she began working undercover as a spy for the Brazilian government's Espionage Network. Beatriz was injured during a mission when a gun powered by a substance named pyroplasm exploded in her hands. Afterward, Bea found she had the ability to create this magical green fire herself. Engulfing her body in pyroplasm flames at will, Beatriz can fly, phase through objects, and set obstacles alight.

Beatriz is hot-headed and impulsive, but her instincts in times of danger are usually correct. She is a good match for her chilled-out, crime-fighting partner and best friend, Tora Olafsdotter, also known as Ice. Together, Beatriz and Tora are part of Justice League International, a Super Hero team sponsored by the United Nations. Beatriz is Brazil's most famous Super Hero.

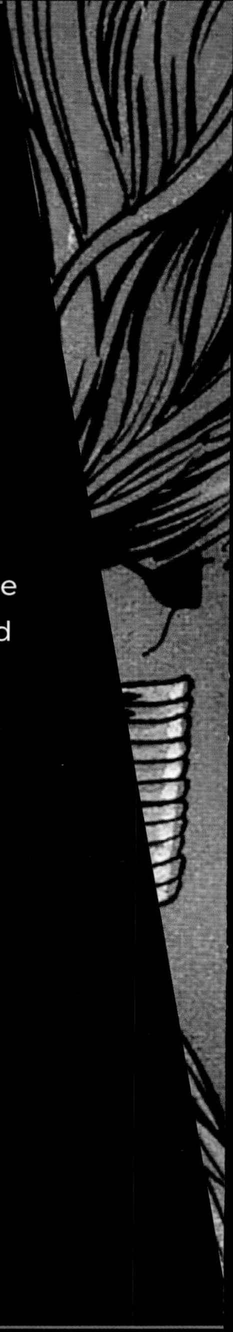

DATA FILE

Friends and allies: Vixen (p14), Ice (p28)

Place of birth: Rio de Janeiro, Brazil

Special skills: Fluent in Portuguese, Spanish, and English

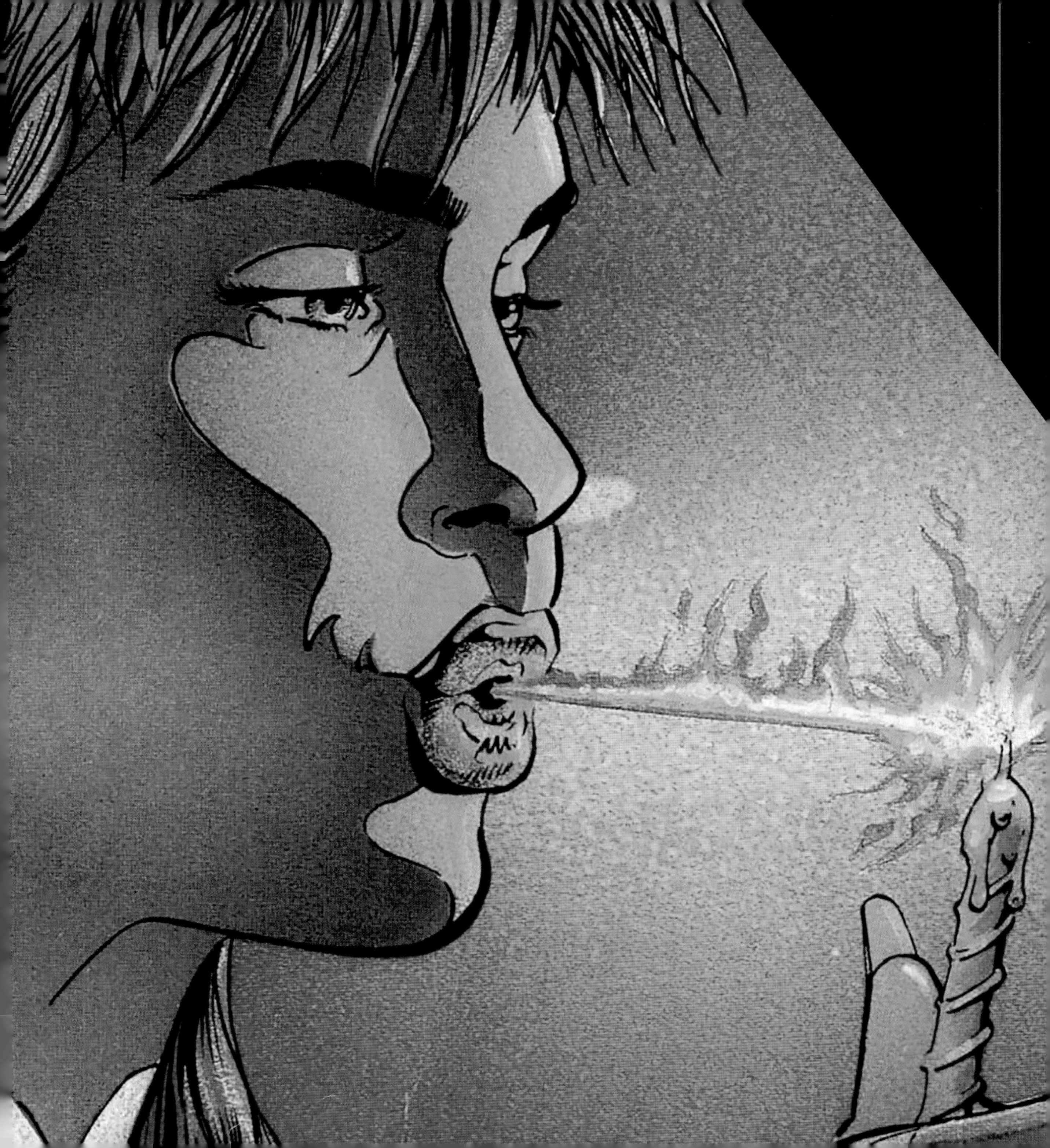

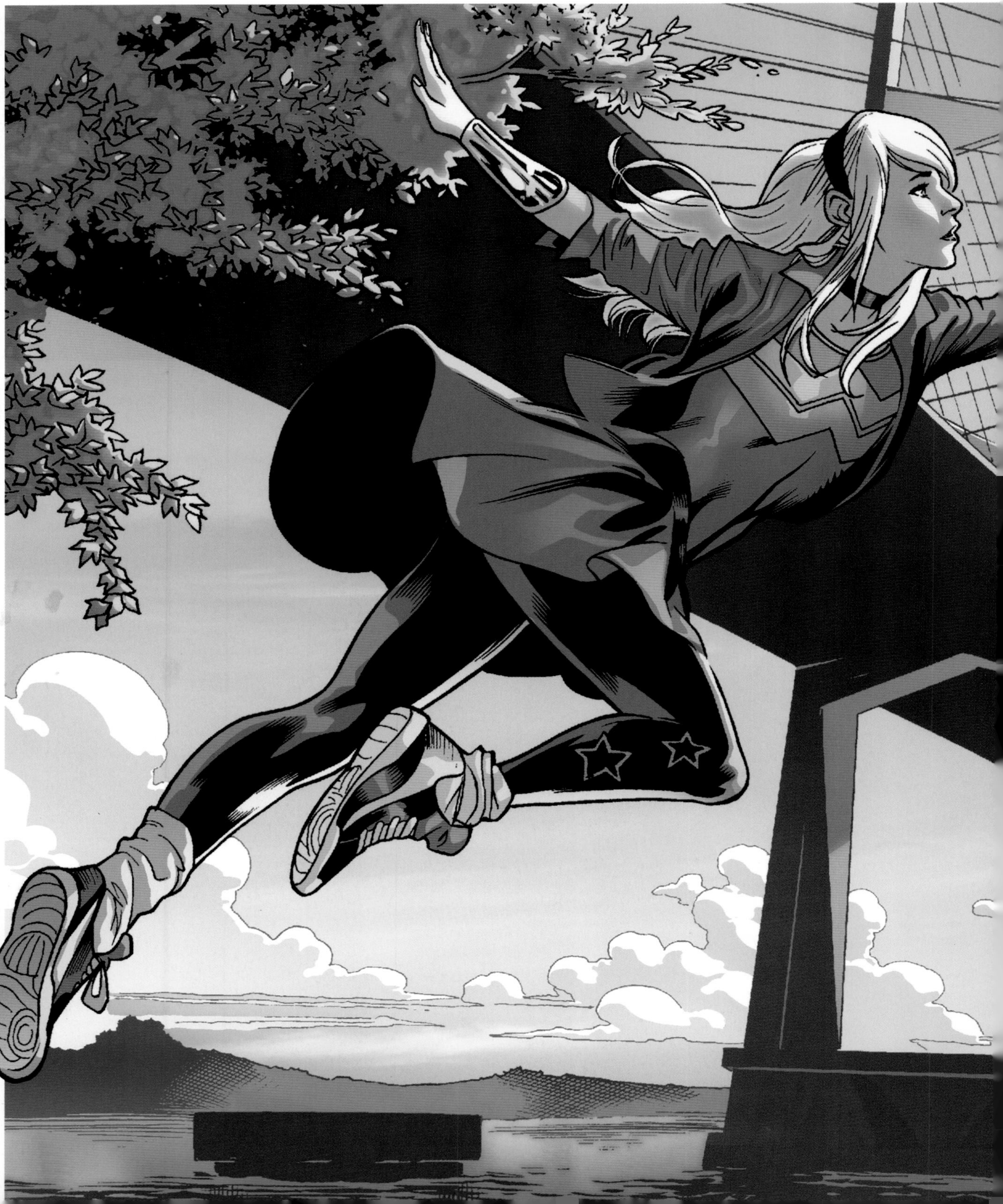

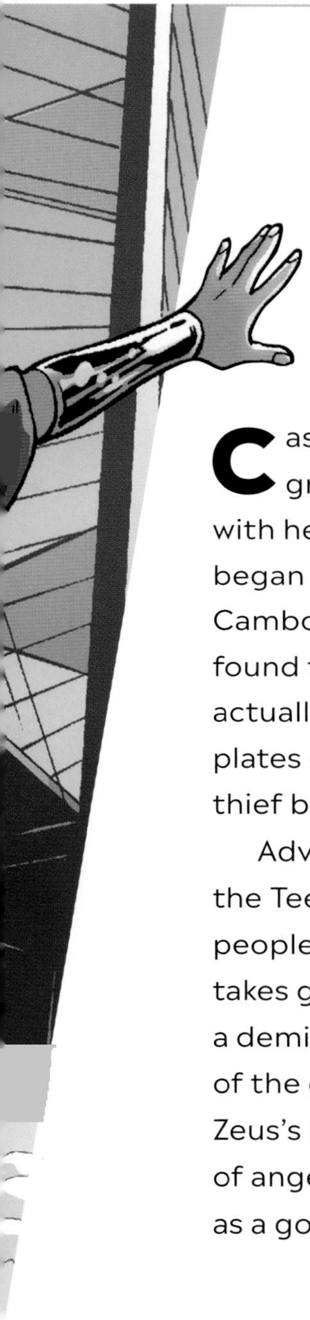

WONDER GIRL

"We do this to help people, right? Save lives."

Cassandra Sandsmark is one of the god Zeus's granddaughters. She grew up traveling the world with her archaeologist mother. With few friends, Cassie began stealing art to keep herself occupied. On a trip to Cambodia with her mother, Cassie went exploring and found two golden bracelets. These ancient artifacts were actually an alien parasite that covered Cassie in powerful plates called the Silent Armor. This fierce, armor-clad thief became known as Wonder Girl.

Adventurous and independent, Cassie helped found the Teen Titans group. She finds it as challenging to trust people as she does to control her alien armor, which takes great willpower to use. Cassie also has powers as a demigoddess. She can fly and call on the magical energy of the gods. She uses a lariat (a type of lasso) that projects Zeus's lightning, and its power is equal to Cassie's level of anger. With time, Cassie is growing into her potential as a good teammate and leader.

DATA FILE

Friends and allies: Dove (p20), Miss Martian (p22)
Enemies: The Crime Syndicate, Trigon
Special skill: Able to speak all languages

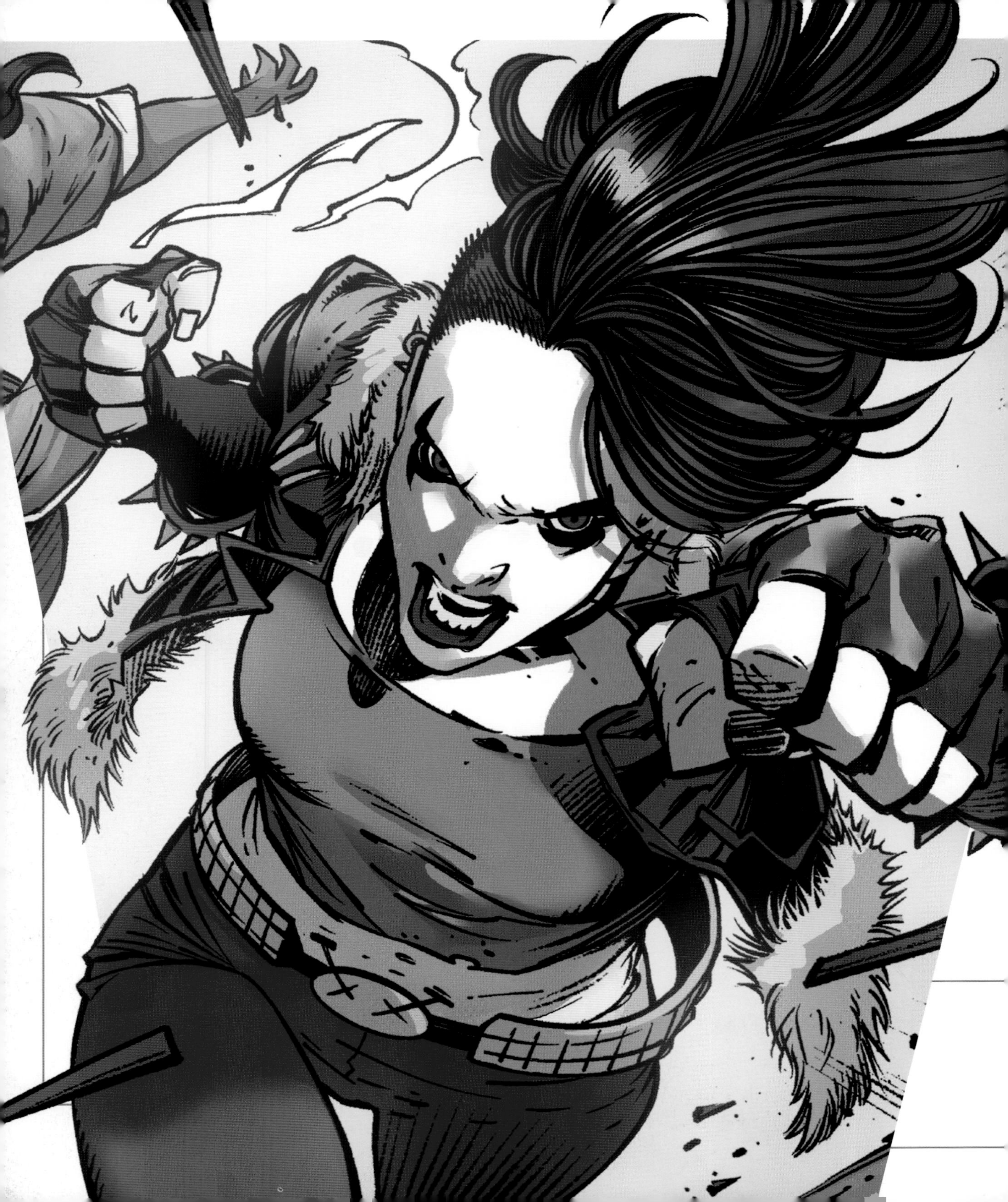

CRUSH

"I'm not sure if this is the bravest thing I've ever seen or the dumbest?"

As a baby, Xiomara fell to Earth wrapped in a living chain called Obelus. She was found and adopted by the Rojas, a couple attending a nearby festival. The Rojas homeschooled Xiomara until they were tragically killed. Tough and determined, she became a competitive fighter called Crush. 15-year-old Xiomara was spotted at a fight by the Super Hero Robin. He recruited Crush into the Teen Titans.

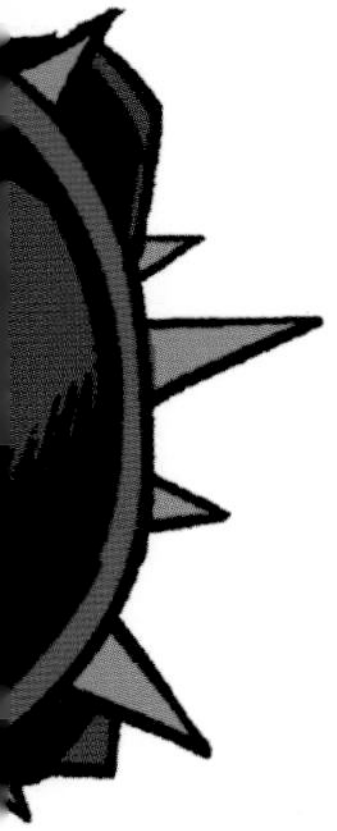

Crush is from the planet Czarnia, whose people are super-strong, fast, and durable. She is fierce in battle, especially when she uses Obelus to fight. The living chain is her constant companion and protector. Though Crush does not like many people, she has lifted buildings and thrown bombs into space to protect her teammates. Crush says exactly what she feels (usually rage). She loves trouble and does not care what people think of her. The Titans are slowly teaching her to trust others. Crush's fashion sense is best described as "heavy metal."

DATA FILE

Friends and allies: Starfire (p104), Emiko Queen (p116)
Enemies: Ezikiel, Brother Blood
Base: Teen Titans HQ, Brooklyn, NY

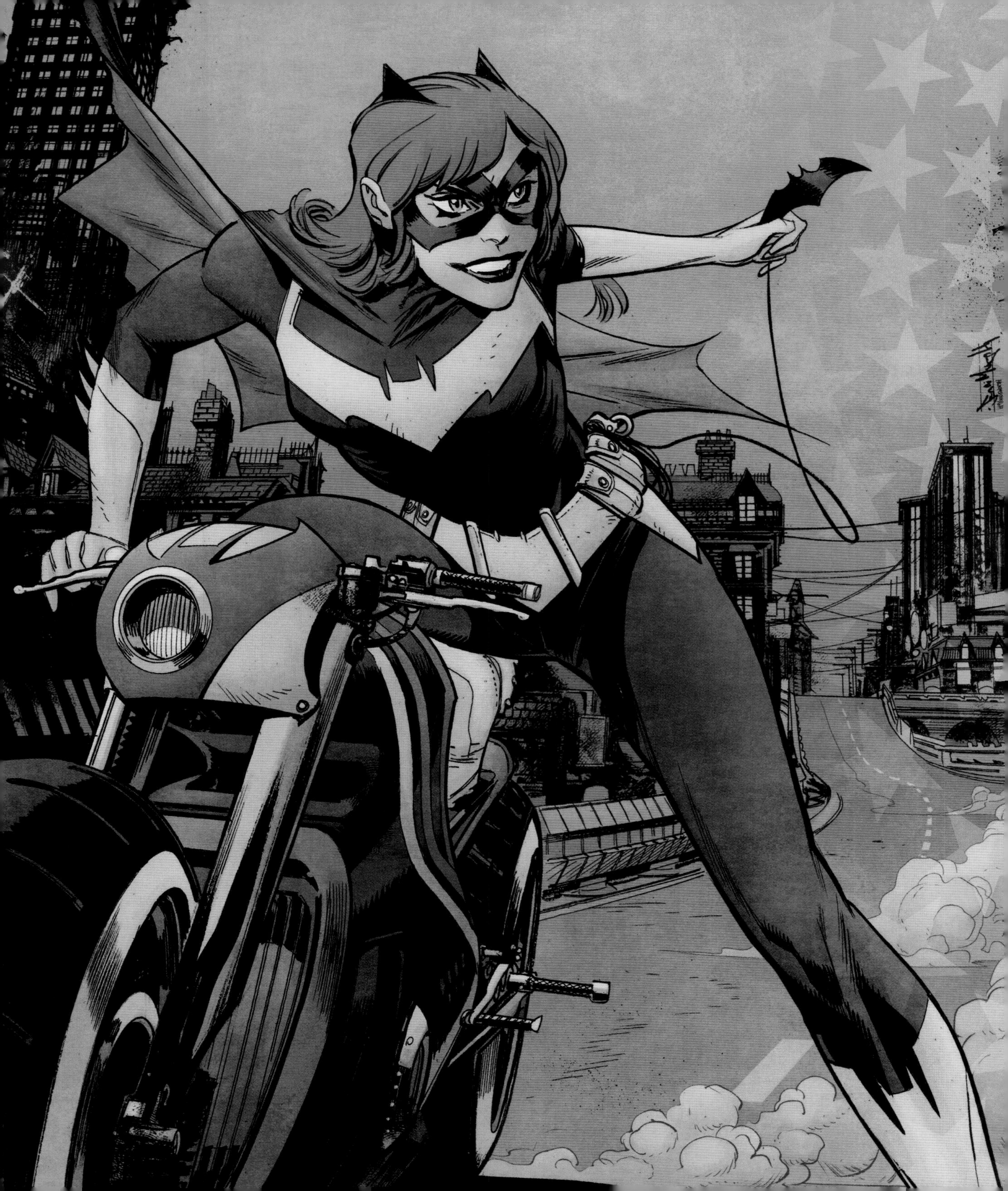

CURIOUS

A Super Hero's mind is just as important a weapon as
her powers. Intelligent, daring heroes such as Batgirl,
a computer whiz, and Lois Lane, a tireless reporter,
solve crimes with science and smarts. Whether they
are good with words, code, math, or metal, these heroes
prove that mind really can triumph over matter.

◀ Batgirl (p72)

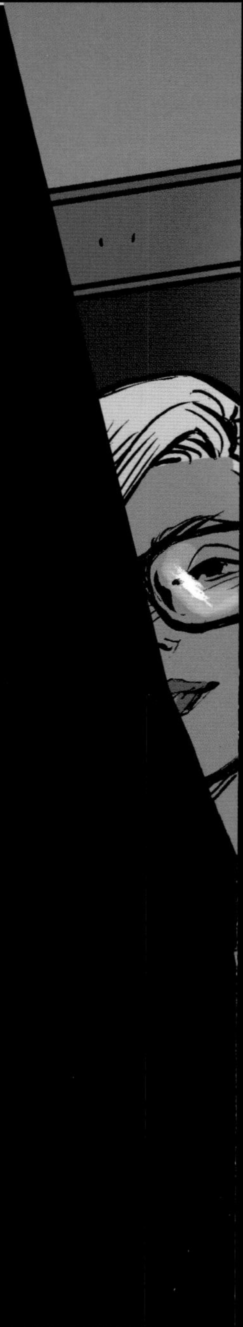

BATGIRL

"I have been given a gift. And it's time to use it. Dear dirtbags... meet Batgirl."

College student Barbara "Babs" Gordon is the Batgirl of Burnside, the coolest neighborhood in Gotham City. Babs first learned about the Super Hero Batman from her father, Police Commissioner Jim Gordon. Inspired by her dad's stories, Babs began fighting alongside Batman. When a serious injury caused Babs to need a wheelchair, she took the opportunity to improve her already-sharp computer hacking skills. Using the name Oracle, Babs founded the all-women crime-fighting group the Birds of Prey. Babs supported the team digitally from their headquarters during missions.

With the help of a special implant, Babs can walk and work as Batgirl again. She keeps Burnside safe from all kinds of dangers—from an evil artificial intelligence to the antihero Harley Quinn. Batgirl stands out from other Bat-heroes with her signature yellow boots, purple leather jacket, and cool motorcycle, the Batcycle. Babs has also started her own green energy business.

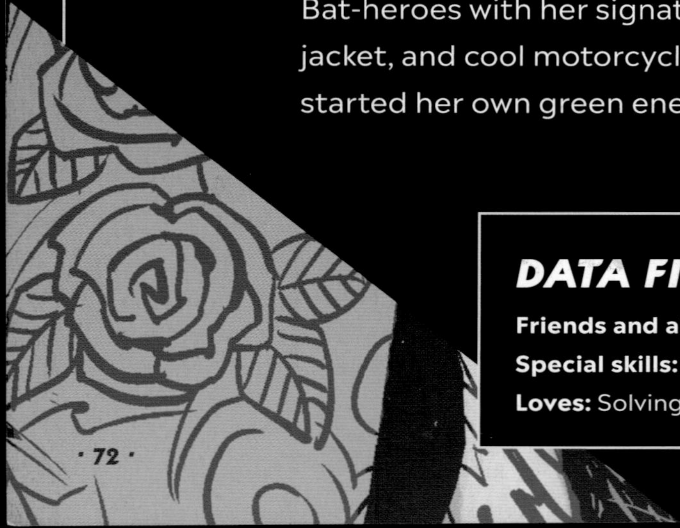

DATA FILE

Friends and allies: Black Canary (p16), Huntress (p40)

Special skills: Martial arts expert, photographic memory

Loves: Solving problems

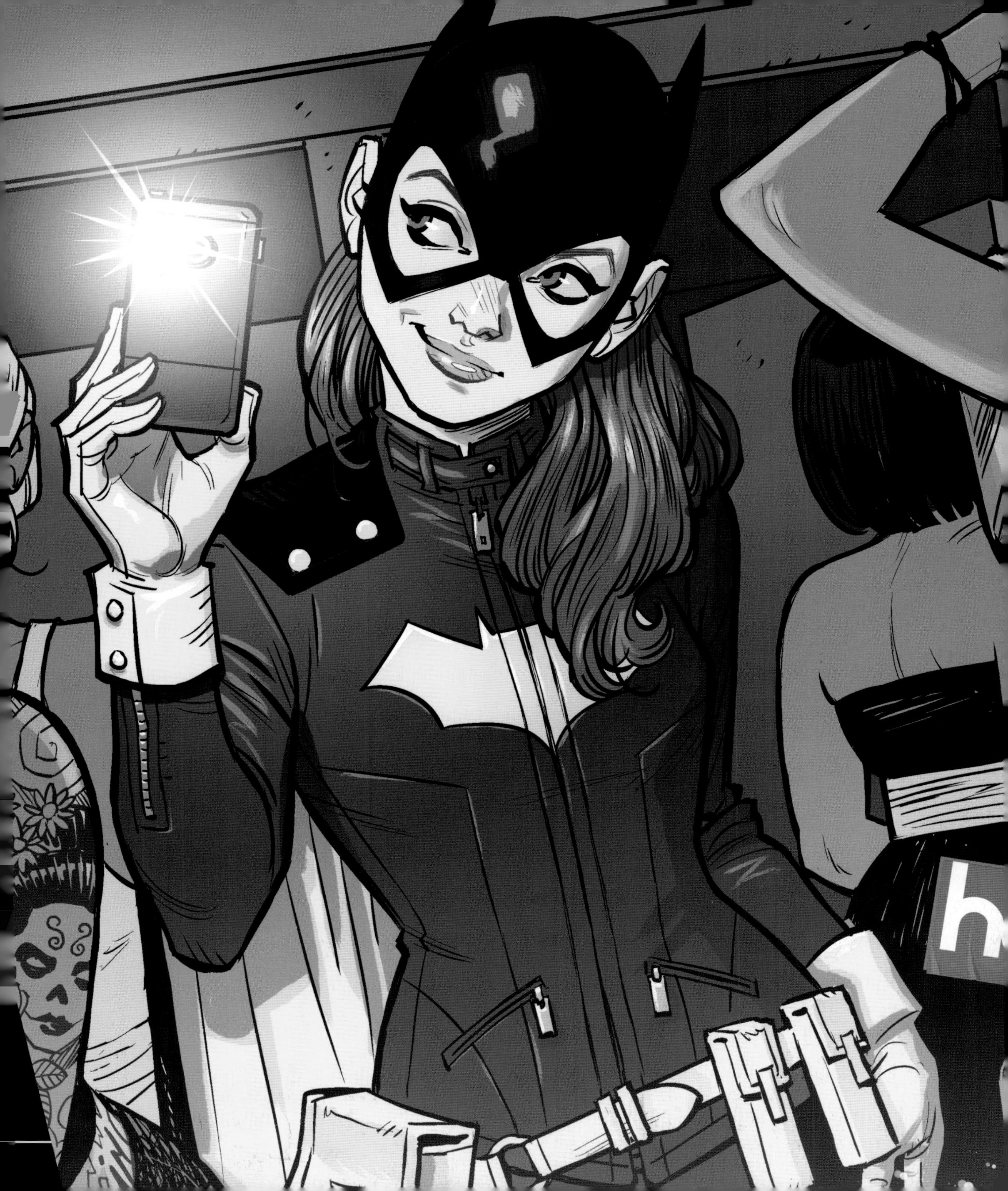

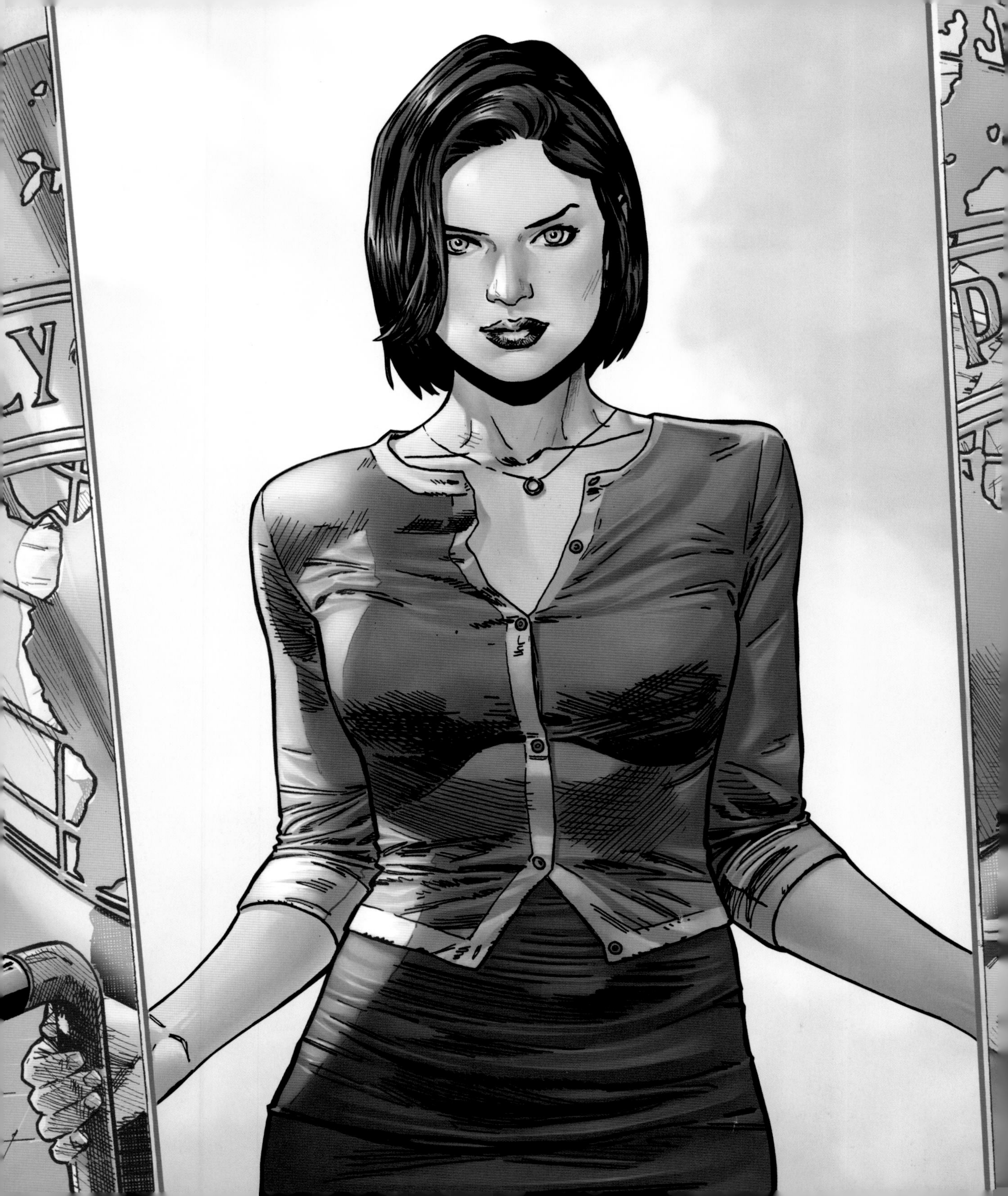

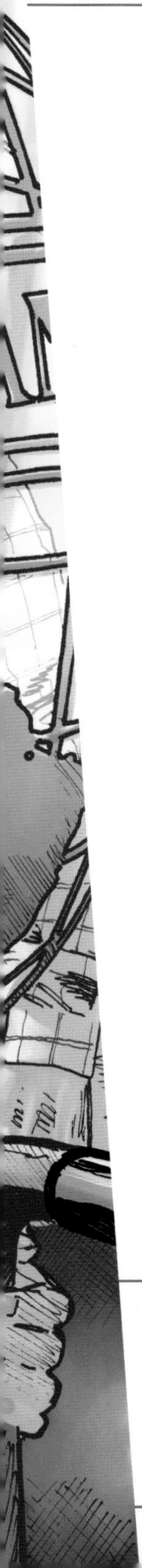

LOIS LANE

"No thug is going to kidnap me! I've worked out with the best!"

Lois Lane is the *Daily Planet* newspaper's best investigative journalist. She has won the paper the highest award in journalism, the Pulitzer Prize. Lois was raised by her military father and has always been tough, pursuing her stories and subjects persistently. She convinced the *Planet*'s editor-in-chief to hire her after she broke into an evil businessman's office to steal secrets. Lois was just 15 at the time.

After Superman saved her from a plane crash, Lois became the first reporter ever to interview him. She was even responsible for being the first to call him Superman in the newspapers. After she learned that Superman was also secretly her coworker Clark Kent, Lois and Clark fell in love and married. Together they work at the *Daily Planet* and have a son, Jonathan Samuel Kent (also known as Superboy). Lois has often shown her own bravery while protecting her family, including fighting in the armor of a Female Fury warrior (like Big Barda) and driving the Batmobile.

DATA FILE

Friends and allies: Supergirl (p32), Lana Lang (p54)
Loves: Reporting, Superman
Enemies: Mister Mxyzptlk, Lex Luthor

HAWKGIRL

"Hey, face... meet MACE!"

In ancient Egypt, the princess Chay-Ara found the remains of an alien spaceship. The spaceship was made of a powerful flight-giving material called Nth Metal. The Nth Metal formed a psychic bond with Chay-Ara, granting her superhuman abilities. Unfortunately, it also trapped her in an endless cycle of death and rebirth. Chay-Ara's most recent incarnation is that of Kendra Saunders, better known as the Super Hero Hawkgirl.

Kendra is a skilled fighter with or without weapons. Her favorite mace (a spiked club) is made from Nth Metal and it can repel all forms of magic. She also has a gravity-defying belt and razor-sharp wings she uses to fly. Kendra was once the creator and leader of the Blackhawks, a secretive team designed to stop world-ending threats. Hawkgirl is now a member of the Justice League team. As one of the oldest humans on Earth, her buildup of knowledge over the centuries has made her as wise as she is strong. Kendra loves driving cars, and has done so since they were invented.

DATA FILE

Friends and allies: Mera (p34), Lady Blackhawk (p46)
Base: Blackhawk Island
Loves: Medieval weapons

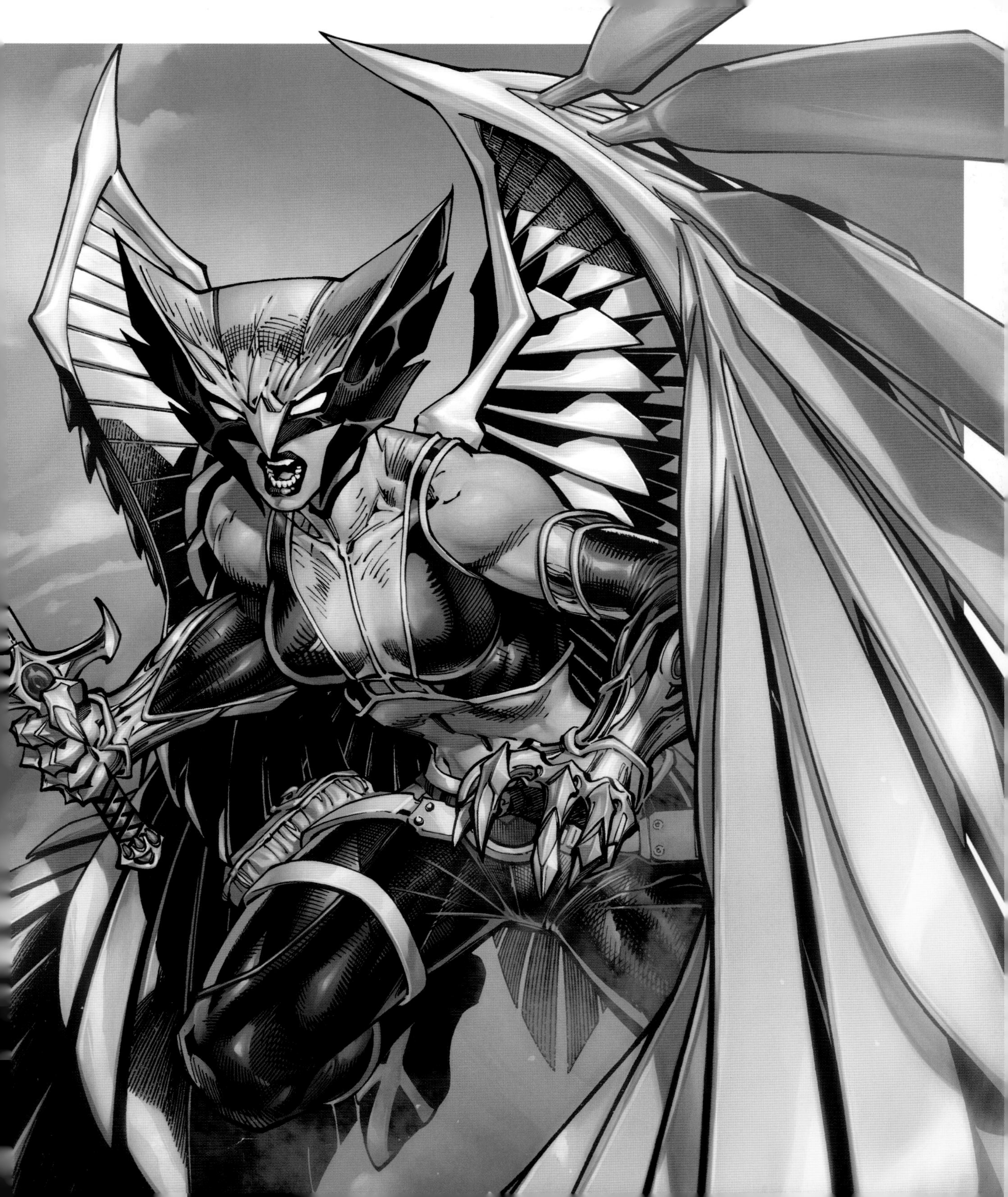

POWER GIRL

"I **don't** have to **imagine**—I'm **living** it.
But I want to be able to **explain** it."

Tanya Spears might just be the smartest teenager in the world. She wanted to become a scientist, like her mother. After finishing her PhD at 17, Tanya carried out her post-doctoral fellowship at the Massachusetts Institute of Technology. She now uses her genius intellect as an intern at Starr Industries, the business run by Karen Starr (also known as Power Girl). With Tanya's help, Power Girl developed a portal between different dimensions. Tanya stood too close to the portal when it closed and became caught up in its energy, receiving superpowers.

Tanya has superhuman strength, and can fly and grow to amazing heights. She has taken on the name Power Girl with Karen's blessing. Tanya does not yet know the extent of her powers and is still discovering new abilities. She has been a part of the Teen Titans and Defiance teams, and has saved the original Power Girl from trouble on more than one occasion. Tanya always wears her hair in her signature buns.

DATA FILE

Friends and allies: Raven (p110), Power Girl—Kara Zor-L (p114)
Place of birth: Boston, MA
Special skill: Lifting up to 3 tons (2,722 kg)

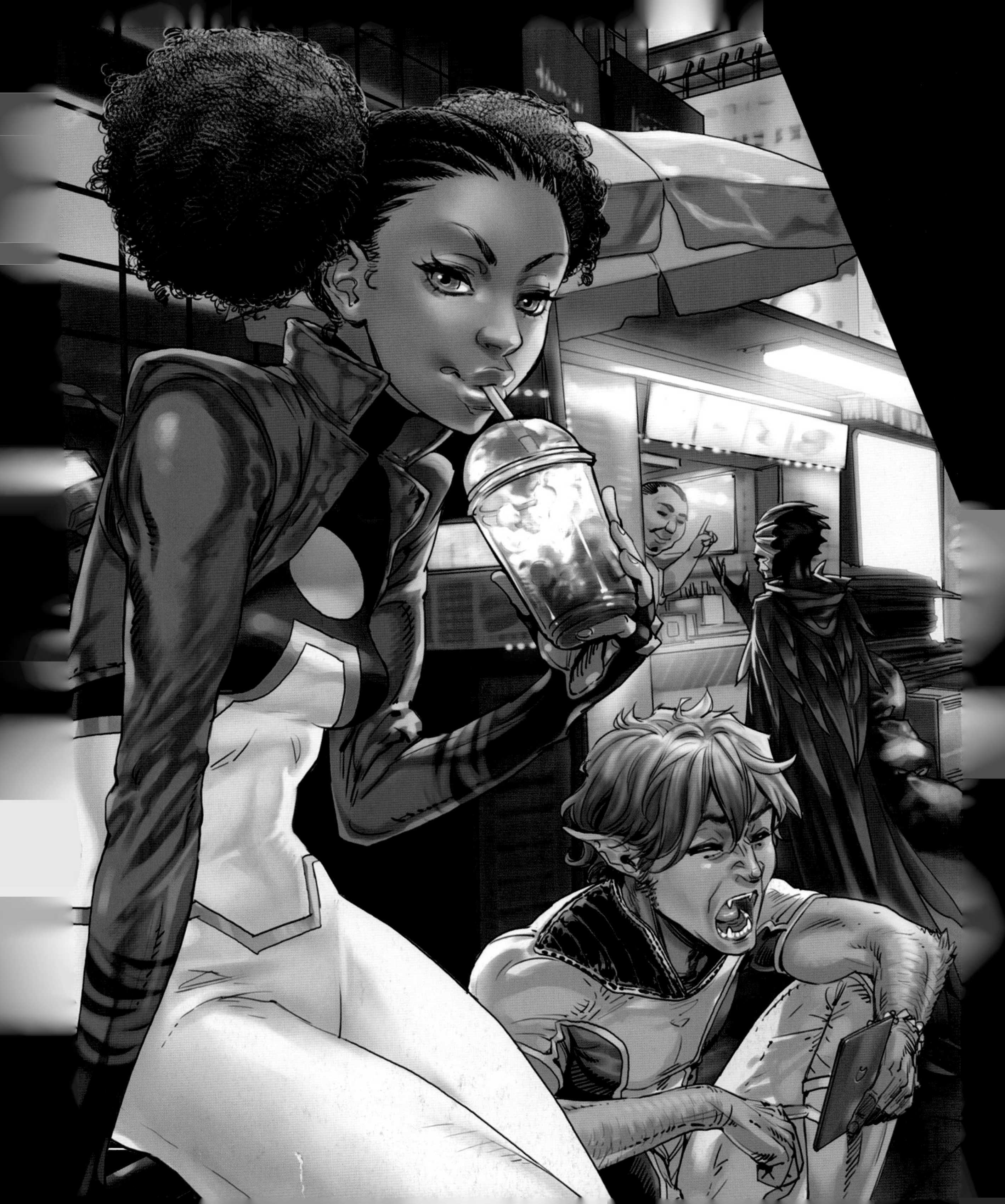

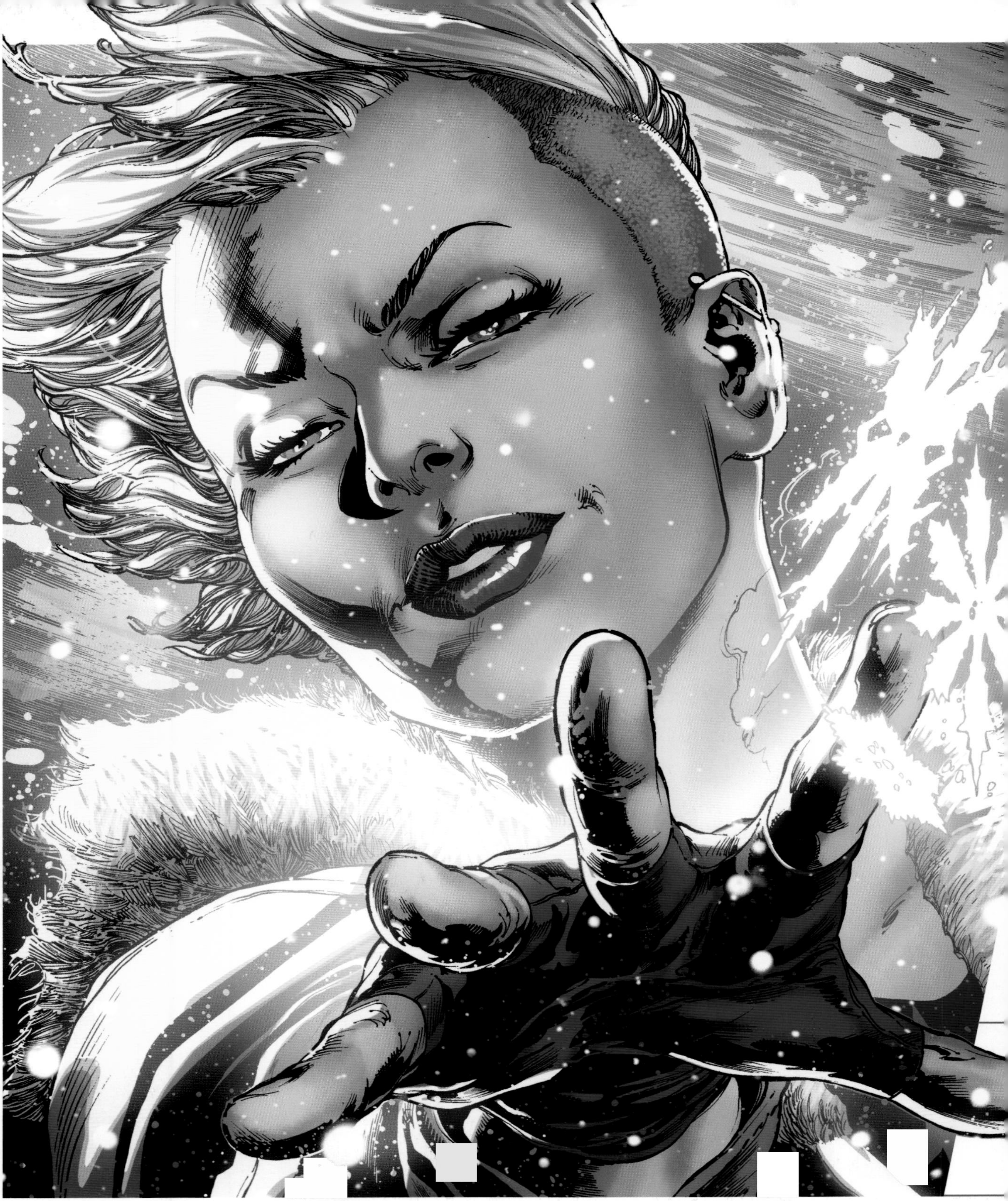

FROST

"It's been **hard,** yeah. It's one thing to **decide** to change, another thing to **do** it."

Caitlin Snow is a brilliant young scientist. She was excited to get a job at S.T.A.R. Labs. Caitlin was working on a special heat engine in the Arctic when S.T.A.R. Labs' jealous business rivals trapped her inside it. While trying to escape, the engine fused Caitlin's very DNA with ice. She gained new abilities, and could create deadly ice shards, dangerous ice storms, and even freeze someone with her touch. Caitlin had to rely on other heat sources to stay alive—usually stealing body heat from other people.

For a while Caitlin was a villain, but later she wanted to change her life and become a better person. She has developed her own suit to help her hold in as much heat as possible. Caitlin has been recruited by Batman to join the Justice League of America, and now fights evildoers as Frost alongside fellow Super Heroes Vixen and Black Canary. Caitlin can have quite a chilly personality, but will warm up to you once you get to know her. Her lips are almost always blue.

DATA FILE

Friends and allies: Vixen (p14), The Flash of China (p52)
Special skill: Solving difficult math equations
Enemy: The Hierarchy of International Vengeance and Extermination (H.I.V.E.)

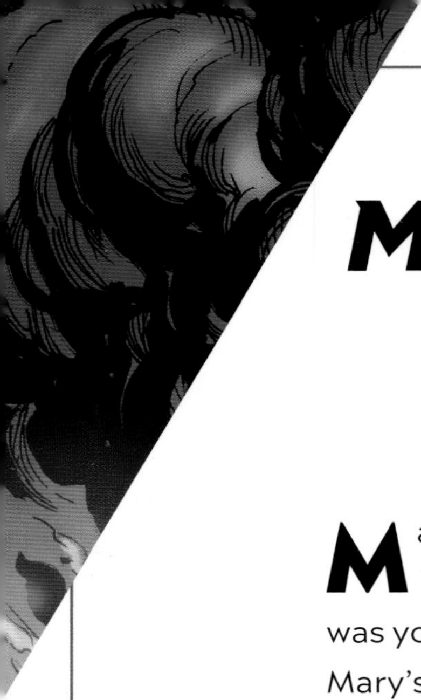

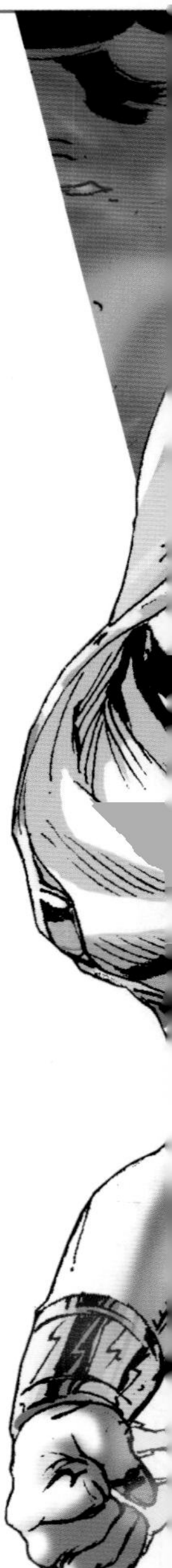

MARY BROMFIELD

"Freddy and Hoppy here are what made this a real home for me."

Mary Bromfield is one of six children fostered by Rosa and Victor Vásquez. Mary ran away from home when she was young, but is now very happy with her foster family. Mary's brother, Billy Batson, was given magical superpowers by a powerful wizard, called Shazam. Billy shares his powers with Mary, and their other siblings, Darla Dudley, Freddy Freeman, Eugene Choi, and Pedro Peña. They transform into adult Super Heroes powered by living lightning when they speak the word "Shazam!" (taken from the names of the supernatural beings Solomon, Hercules, Atlas, Zeus, Achilles, and Mercury).

Alongside her sister and brothers, Mary explores the Seven Magic Realms and defends Earth from the Monster Society of Evil. Mary has a pet rabbit called Hoppy, who she rescued before he could be sent to a lab for cruel cosmetic testing. She is especially close to her younger sister, Darla. Mary is confident and intelligent, and Darla thinks she should be the leader of their family team.

DATA FILE

Friends and allies: Wonder Woman (p12), Darla Dudley (p92)

Base: Philadelphia, PA

Special skills: Electric blasts, super-speed

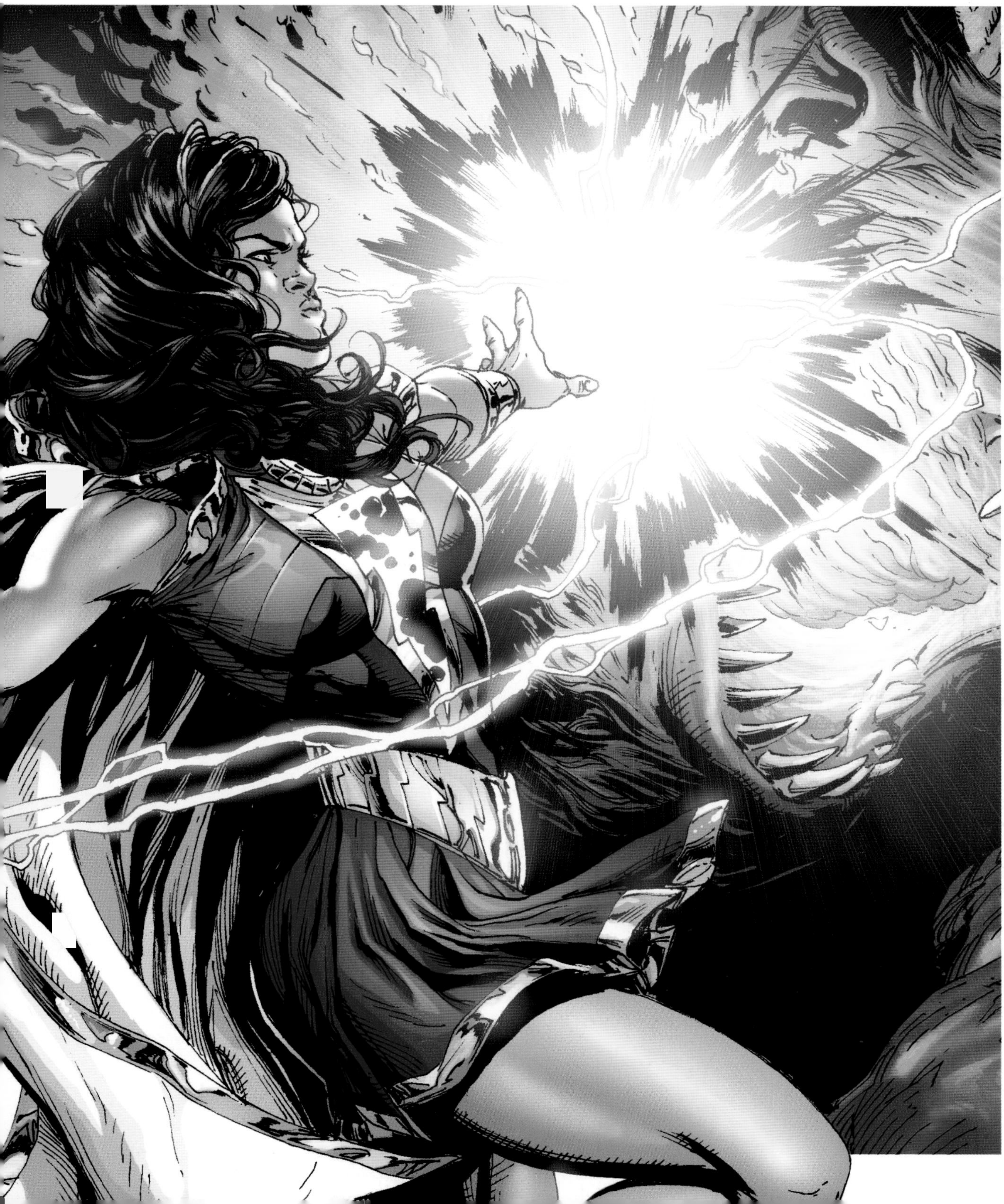

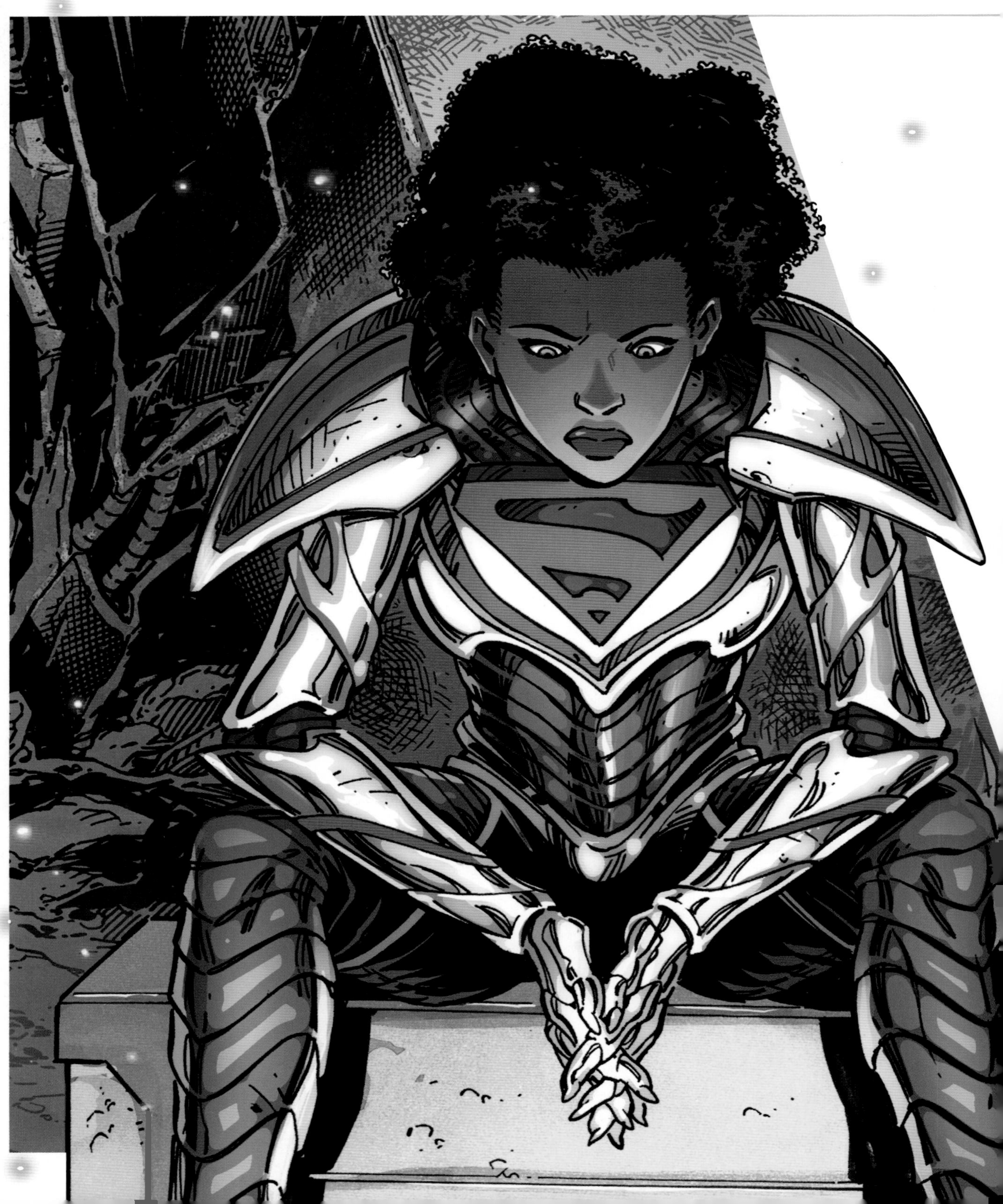

STEEL

"My life will count for something. I will make a difference."

Natasha Irons has super heroism in her family. Her uncle, John Henry, invented a superpowered suit of armor that he used to fight evil. He eventually passed the suit down to his niece. In her suit of liquid, partially-living metal, Natasha is nearly invulnerable and possesses superhuman strength. The suit also allows her to fly and to grow as large as 60 feet tall (over 18 meters).

Natasha's weapon of choice is a kinetic hammer that gains power the longer it flies. It can create powerful electrical fields and can only be used by someone who shares her DNA. Natasha previously interned for a US senator, worked for the businessman Lex Luthor, and dated the magical Traci Thirteen. Now going by the name Steel, Natasha is a member of the Titans Super Hero group, though she has also been known as both Starlight and Vaporlock. For fun, she once reprogrammed Superman's ultra-polite Kryptonian robot to speak in casual slang.

DATA FILE

Friends and allies: Lana Lang (p54), Donna Troy (p62)
Base: The Steelworks, Metropolis
Occupations: Student, inventor

THUNDER

"Hey, I'm kind of invulnerable right now."

Anissa Pierce is the oldest daughter of Jefferson Pierce, the Super Hero Black Lightning. Like her sister Jennifer, Anissa inherited some of her father's superpowers. Anissa can increase the density of her body, making herself extremely heavy. Her punches are weighty, and she can create huge shockwaves by landing on top of an enemy or stomping the ground. In this super-dense form, Anissa is nearly invulnerable—she is even immune to bullets.

Considerate and intelligent, Anissa promised her father that she would finish her education before following in his footsteps as a hero. She successfully completed medical school before she became the crime fighter Thunder. Anissa joined The Outsiders, a secretive team who take on crime-fighting jobs that the Justice League cannot be seen doing. Like Anissa herself, The Outsiders do not care about what the public thinks of them. Anissa lives with her girlfriend and fellow Outsider Grace Choi, an Amazon. Anissa used to fight crime in a blond wig but has reconsidered that fashion choice.

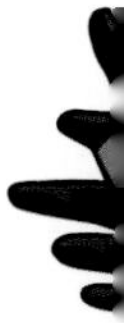

DATA FILE

Friends and allies: Lightning (p42), Starfire (p104)
Occupations: Doctor, adventurer
Special skill: Fluent in French

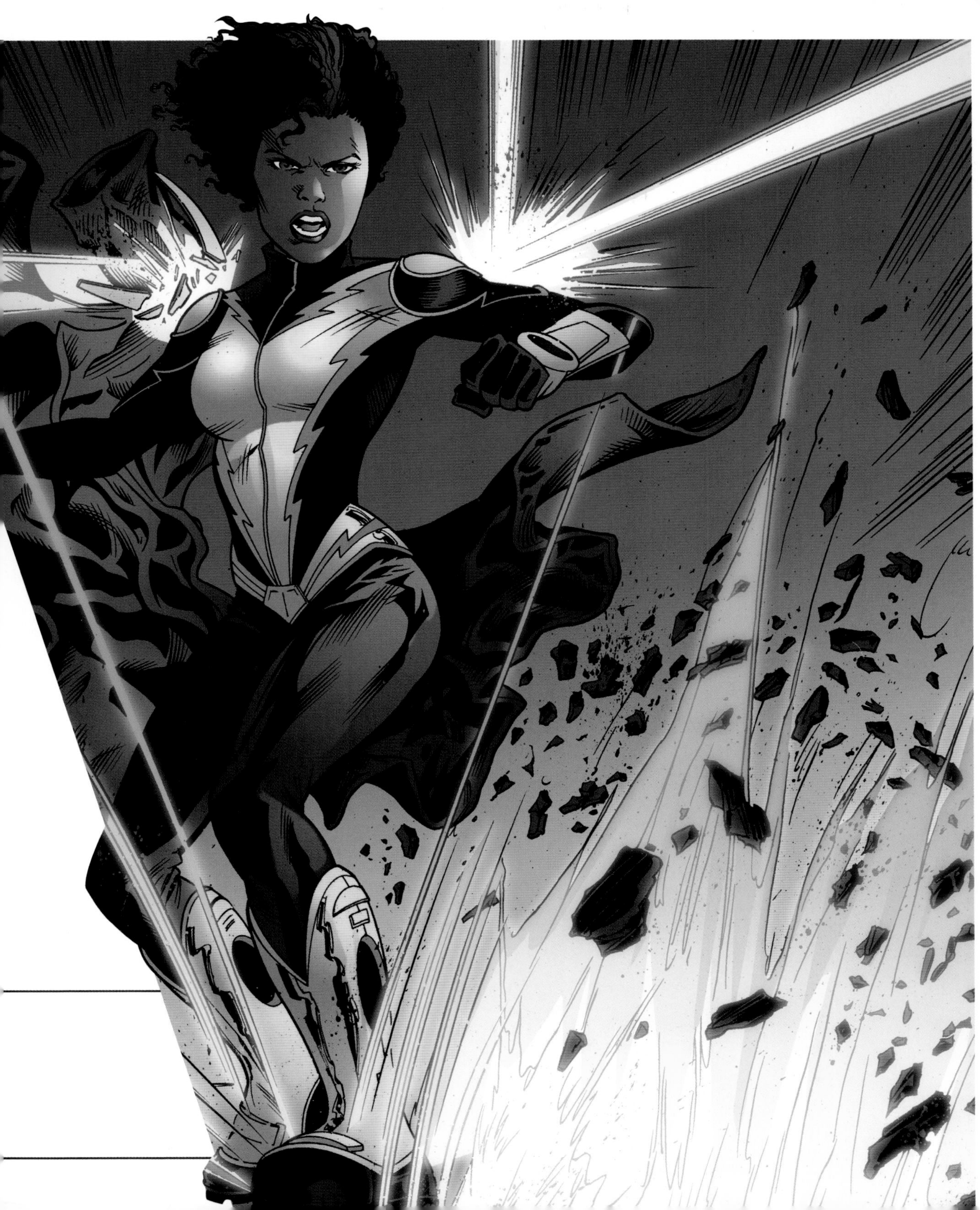

BLUEBIRD

"Sometimes all it takes is a few words to change your life."

Harper Row is from the Narrows, a low-income neighborhood in Gotham City. She was responsible for raising her younger brother on her own. Skillful with gadgets, teenage Harper got a job as an electrical engineer for the city. When she and her brother were attacked by street bullies, they were rescued by the Super Hero Batman. Impressed with Harper's skills, Batman asked her to improve his technology and gadgets. Batman became Harper's mentor.

Instead of taking on the Robin identity like many of Batman's previous sidekicks, Harper uses the name Bluebird. She is a skilled kickboxer and once saved Batman's life using just a car battery and jumper cables. Her personal motto, passed on from her mother before her death, is "Resolve." Now, Harper attends Gotham University to get her official degree in electrical engineering. Harper also volunteers at Dr. Leslie Thompkins' medical clinic for criminals. She sports a purple-and-blue undercut, and has a big crush on Batwoman.

DATA FILE

Friends and allies: Batwoman (p96), Orphan (p112)
Loves: Volunteering, kickboxing
Base: Gotham City

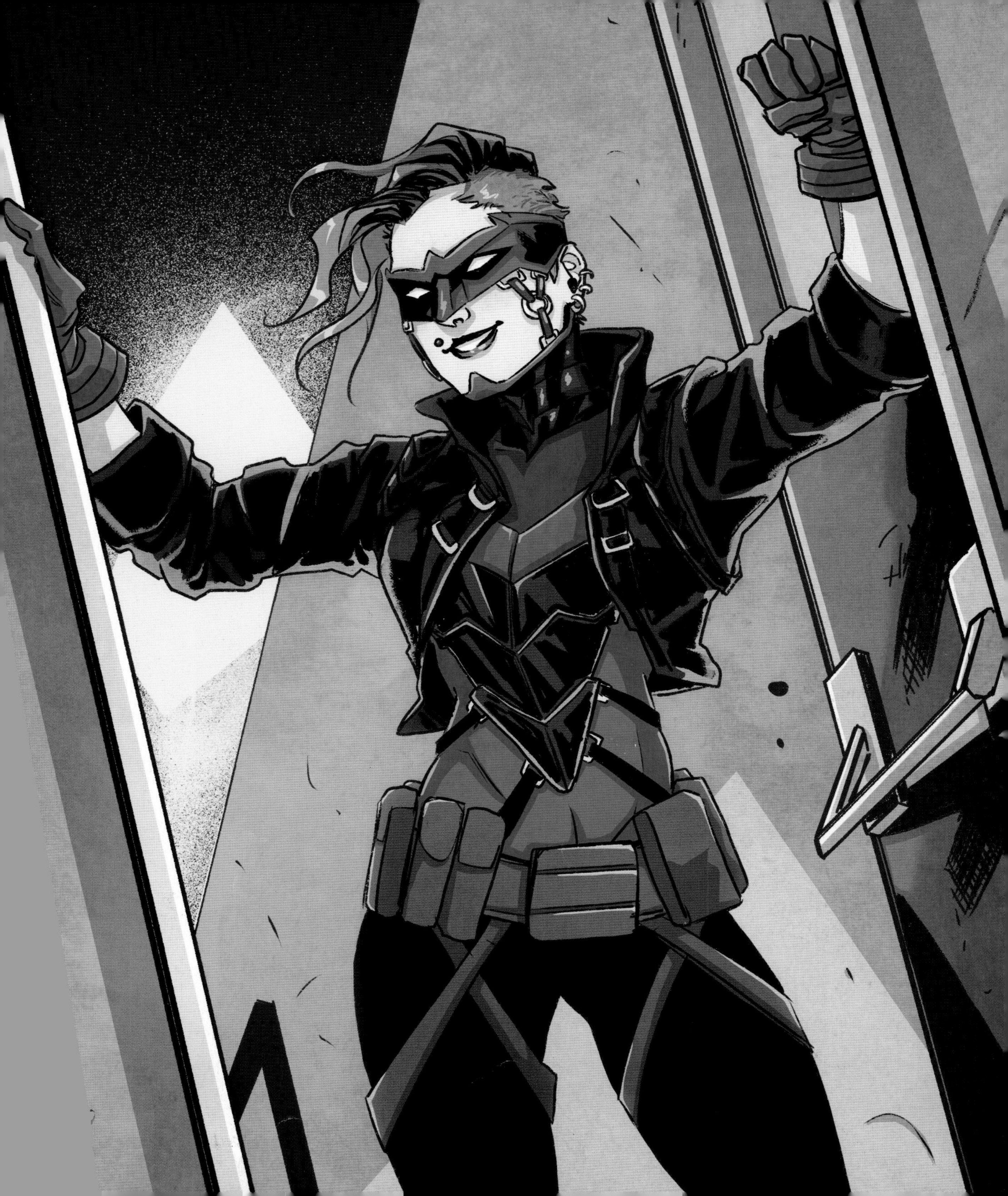

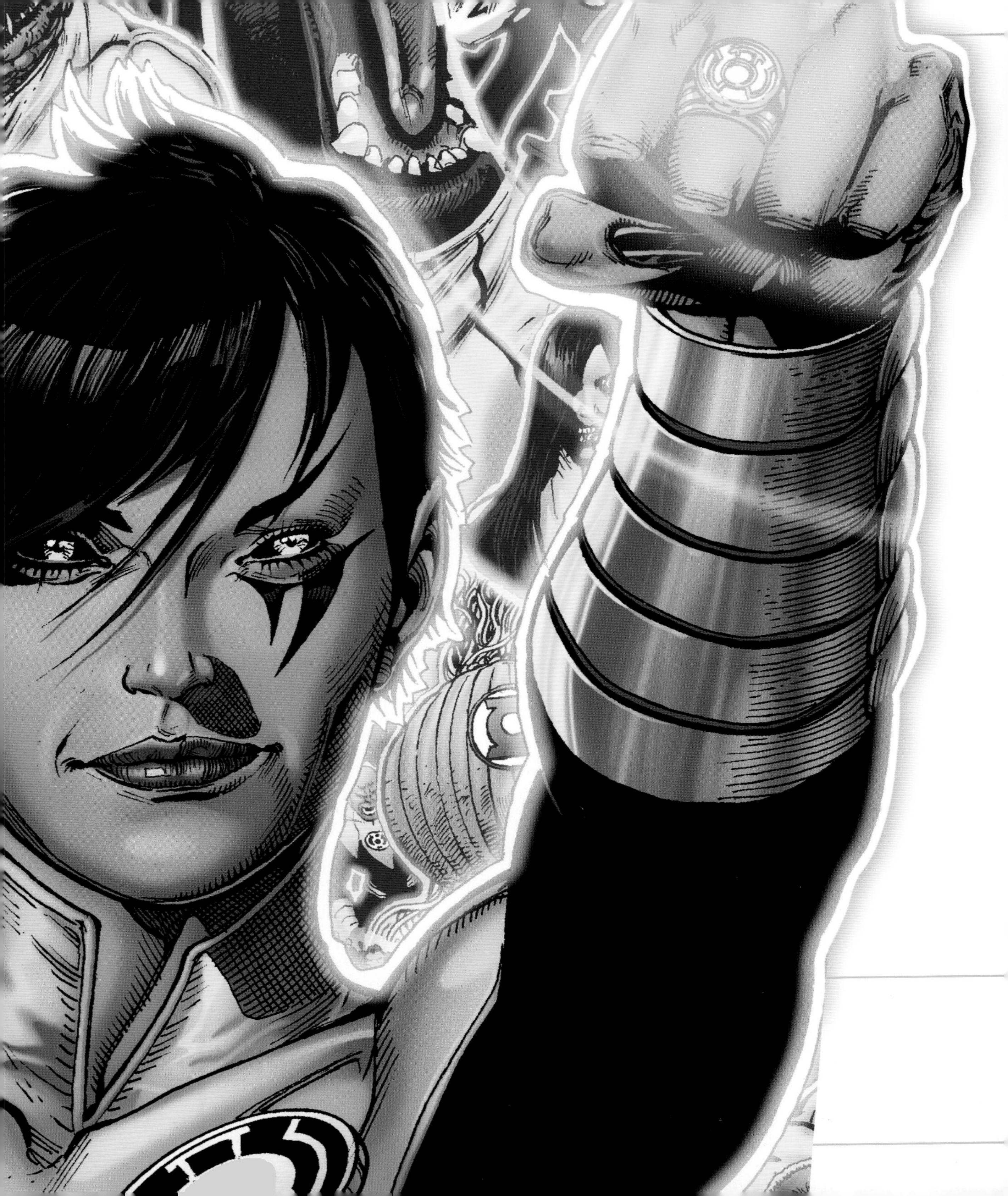

SORANIK NATU

"I am not afraid. And I have **never** **failed** a test in my life."

Soranik Natu is an alien from the planet Korugar. Her cruel father Sinestro once ruled Korugar with a power ring. Another one of these rings chose Soranik to wield its power. This ring came to Soranik, a brilliant neurosurgeon, while she was working on a difficult medical operation. She used the ring to save her patient's life. Soranik promised to use her ring more responsibly than her father did. She became a Green Lantern peacekeeper and defender of Sector 1417, including Korugar.

Like all Green Lanterns, Soranik channels her willpower through her ring. She can fly and project energy into any object she can imagine. Though Soranik is stubborn and bad-tempered, she is secretly soft at heart. She would do anything to protect her people and uses her wisdom to heal those who are hurting. To best protect the universe, Soranik has forged an alliance between her father's Sinestro Corps (also known as the Yellow Lantern Corps) and the Green Lantern Corps.

DATA FILE

Friends and allies: Star Sapphire (p26), Green Lantern (p98)
Occupation: Leader of the Sinestro Corps
Special skills: Healing, interplanetary diplomacy

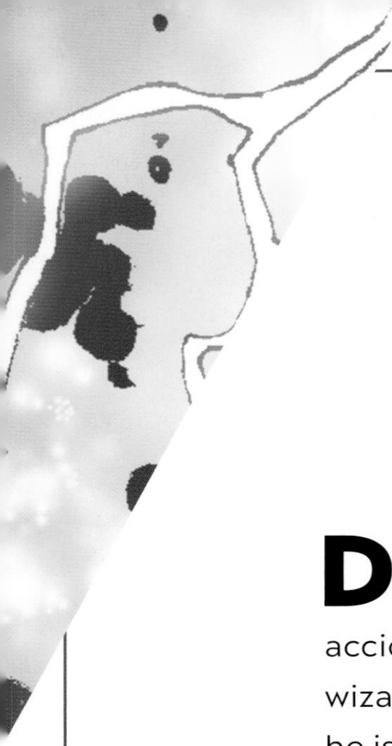

DARLA DUDLEY

"I hope we make some new friends!"

Darla Dudley is one of Victor and Rosa Vásquez's foster children. Darla's foster brother, Billy Batson, accidentally inherited the name and powers of a powerful wizard named Shazam. When Billy speaks the word "Shazam!", he is transformed into an adult with super-speed, strength, and stamina, powered by living lightning. Now Darla and her other foster siblings—Mary, Freddy, Eugene, and Pedro—all share these powers with Billy.

Known together as the Shazam Family, Darla and her siblings fight crime and keep their city safe. Though they are just children, they are very brave and try their best to do the right thing. Darla is very inquisitive and good-natured. Unlike her sister and brothers, when Darla first said the word "Shazam!" she gained superpowers but did not transform. Darla is closest of all to her foster sister, Mary, and looks up to her as both a best friend and a mentor. Darla wears a purple uniform when she is powered up and is the fastest of all the Shazam Family.

DATA FILE

Friends and allies: Wonder Woman (p12), Mary Bromfield (p82)

Enemy: The Monster Society of Evil

Loves: Her foster family, reading

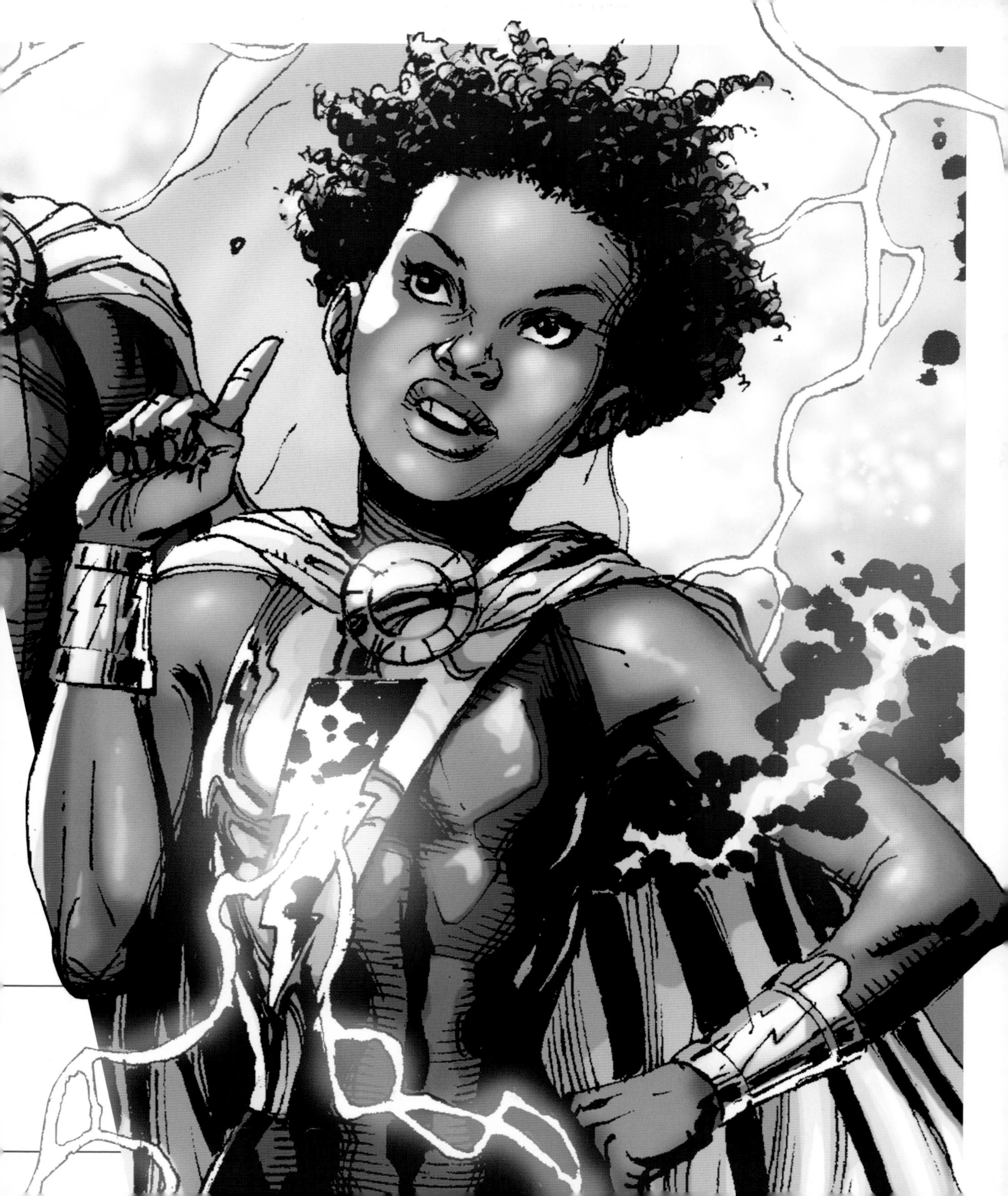

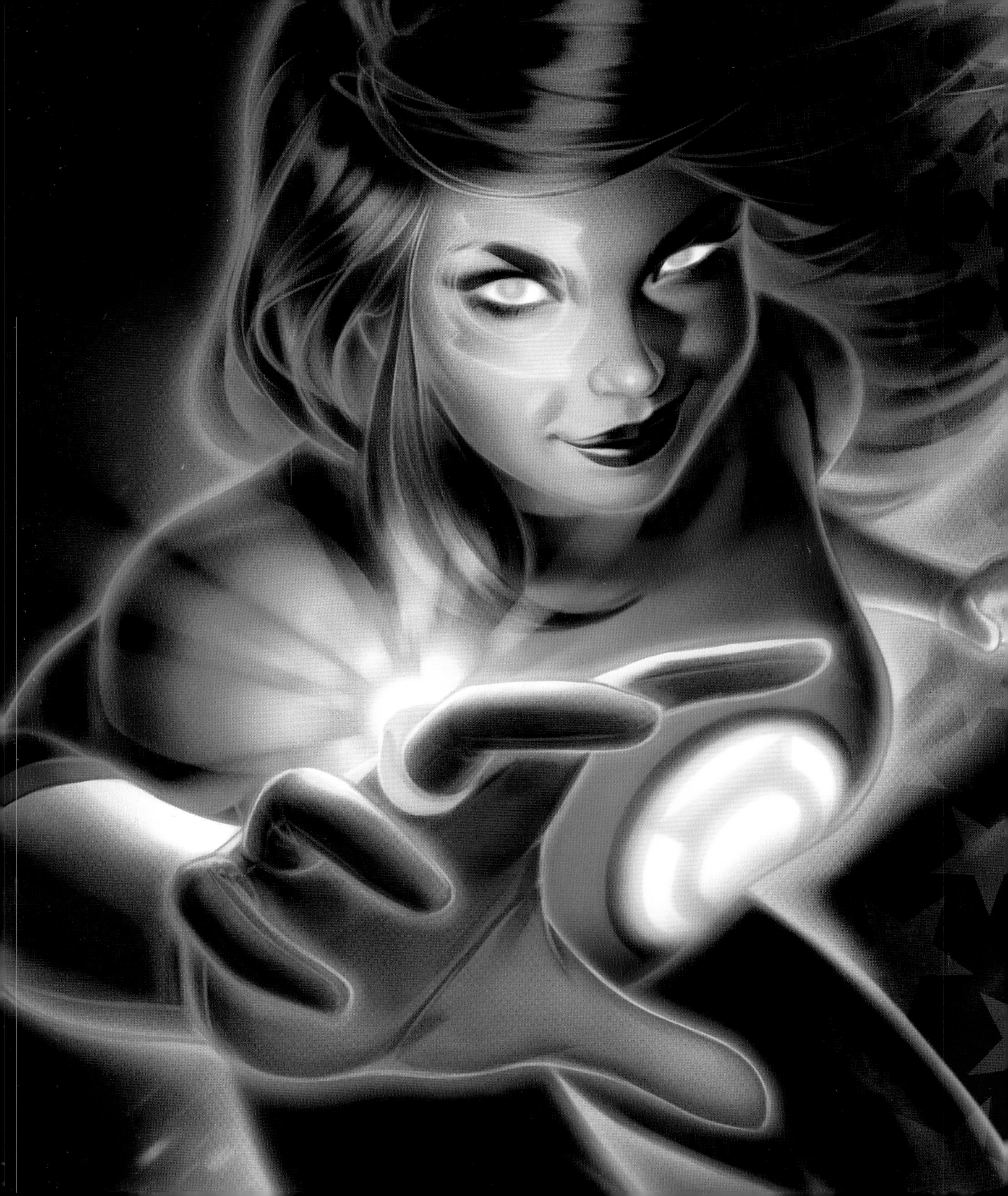

PERSISTENT

A true hero never backs down, no matter how difficult things become. There is no doubt that these determined heroes face great challenges, such as Raven taking on her demonic father, or Elasti-Woman coming to terms with her uncontrollable powers. But these heroes always get back up, no matter how many times the world tries to knock them down.

◄ Green Lantern (p98)

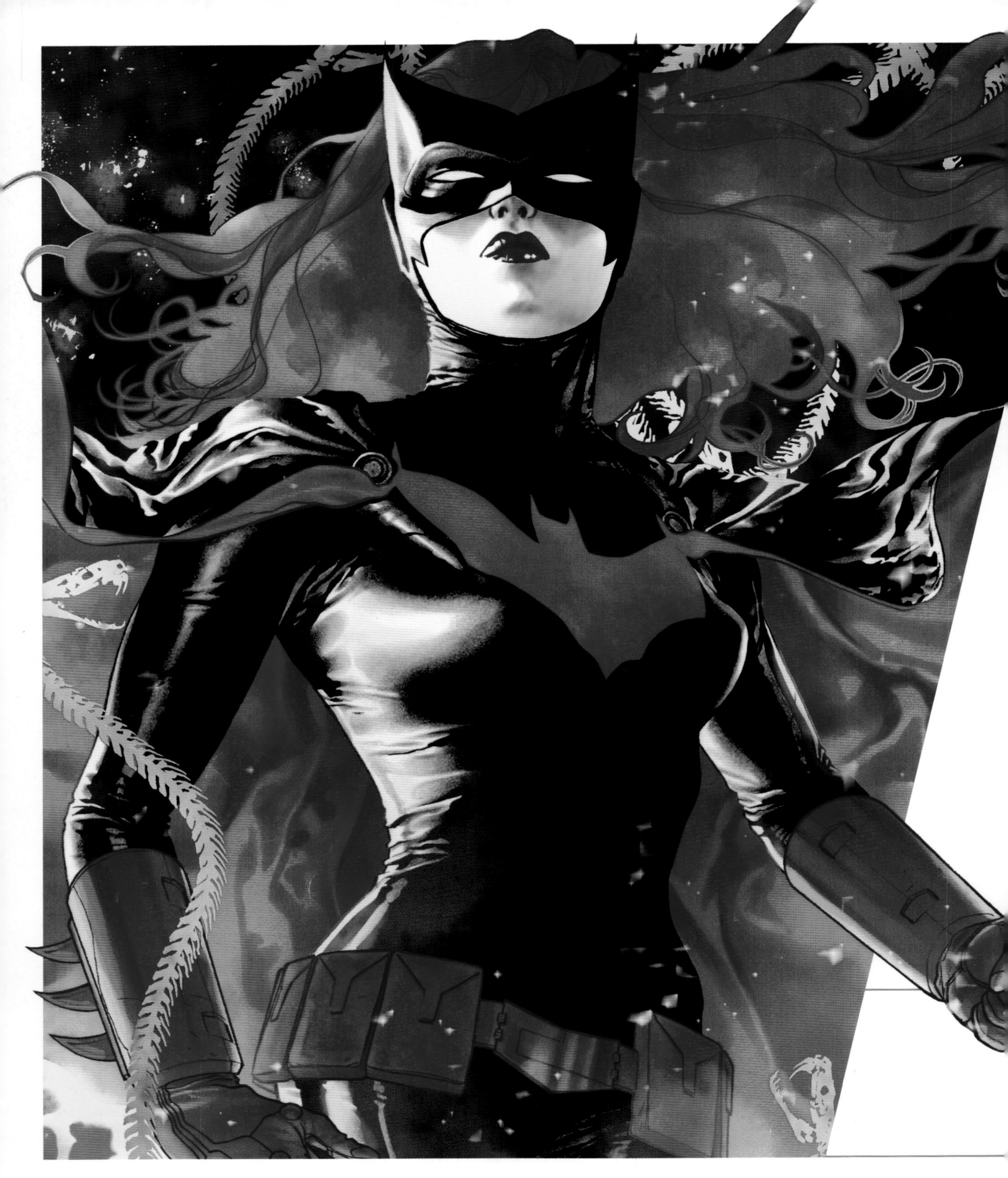

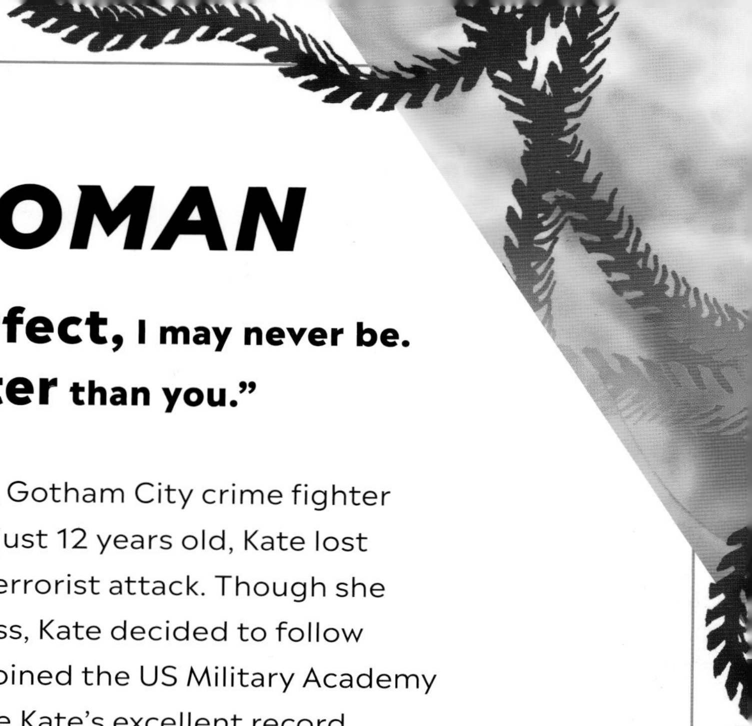

BATWOMAN

"I might not be perfect, I may never be. But I'm better than you."

Kate Kane is the redheaded, Gotham City crime fighter Batwoman. When she was just 12 years old, Kate lost her mother and her sister in a terrorist attack. Though she was an incredibly wealthy heiress, Kate decided to follow in her mother's footsteps and joined the US Military Academy in West Point, New York. Despite Kate's excellent record and multiple awards, she was expelled for being gay.

Kate moved to Gotham City. While defending herself from muggers, Kate was helped by her cousin, the Super Hero Batman. Inspired by his work, Kate decided to use her fortune to fight back against evil. Famously no-nonsense, Kate is a skilled investigator and fighter. She uses Batarangs (bat-shaped throwing knives), taser gloves, and a personalized motorcycle called the Red Knight One. Her long red wig is attached to her cowl. Kate and Gotham City Police detective Renee Montoya have an on-again, off-again relationship. Kate is a fan of rock music and plays the guitar.

DATA FILE

Friends and allies: Renee Montoya (p58), Zatanna (p60)
Loves: The rock bands Blondie and The Sisters of Mercy
Occupations: Socialite, charity supporter

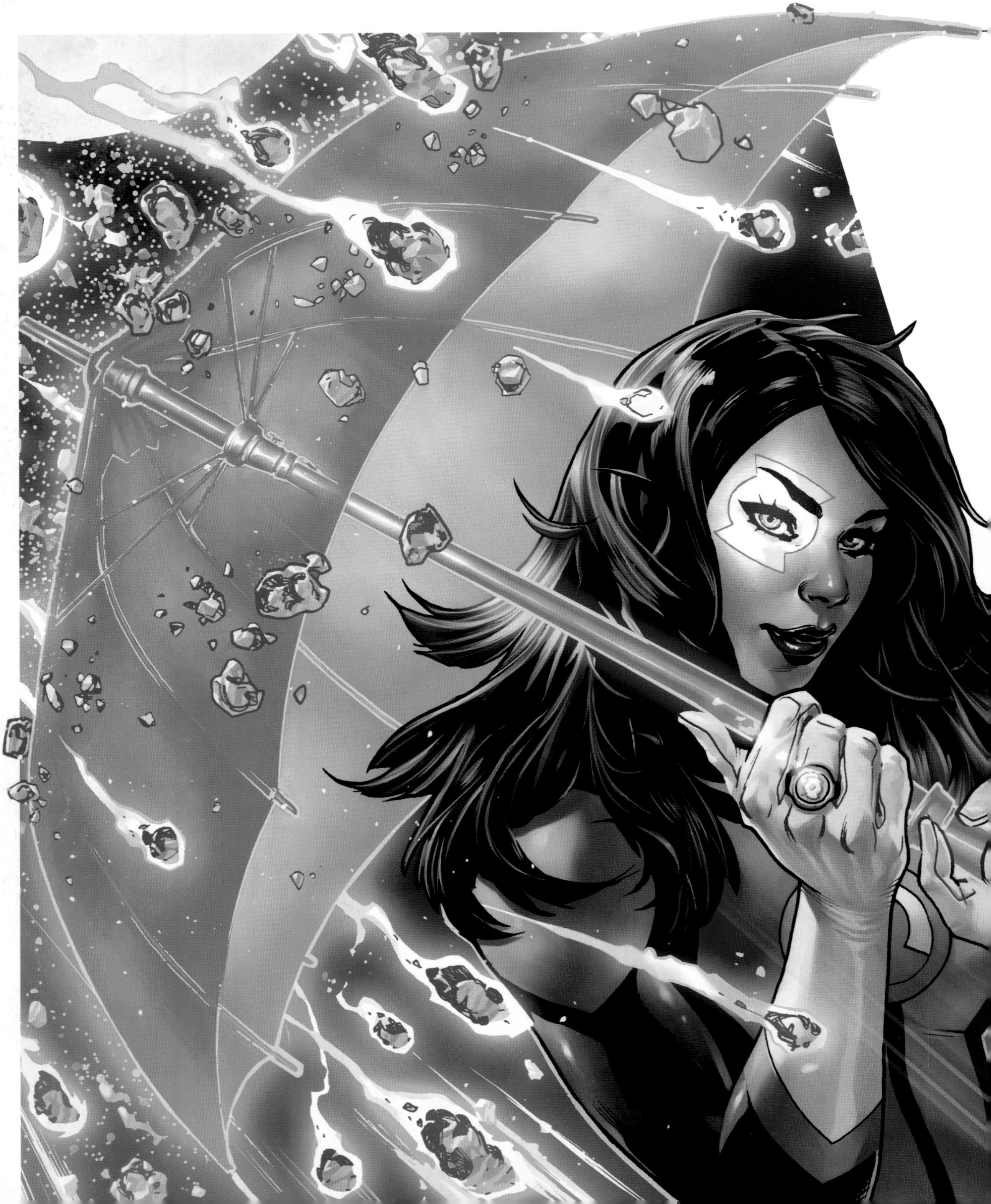

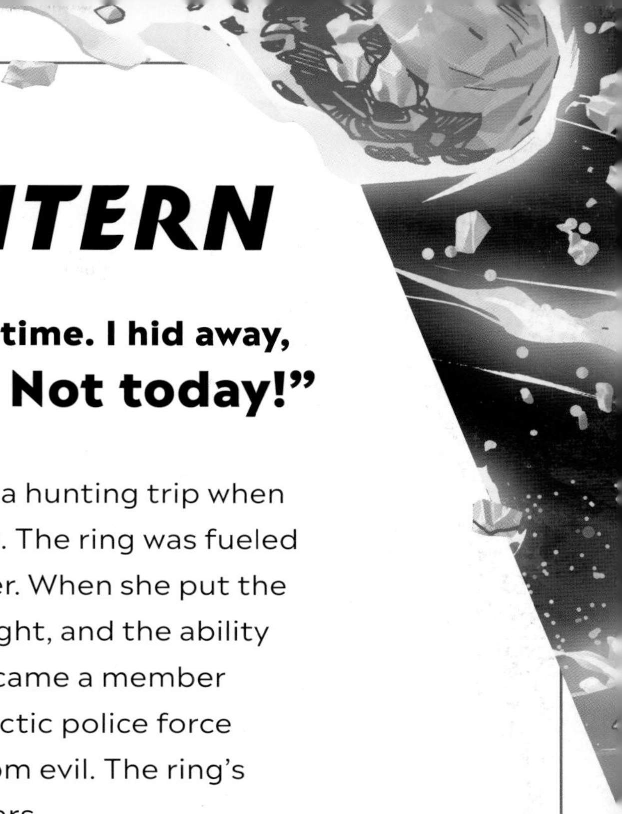

GREEN LANTERN

"I used to be scared all the time. I hid away, too frightened to do anything... Not today!"

Jessica Cruz was just a regular girl on a hunting trip when she found a power ring in the woods. The ring was fueled by the green-colored energy of willpower. When she put the ring on, Jessica received the power of flight, and the ability to create and project energy. Jessica became a member of the Green Lantern Corps, an intergalactic police force dedicated to protecting the universe from evil. The ring's power is limited only by Jessica's own fears.

Jessica has since been paired up with other Green Lanterns on Earth and in outer space to defeat many villains, including Darkseid and the Black Racer. Together, the Green Lanterns try to conquer their greatest enemy: the yellow-colored energy of fear. Jessica does not always find this easy and sometimes calls herself the "anxiety Lantern." However, she works hard to overcome her anxious feelings and to find her inner strength. At home on Earth, Jessica is a citizen of both Mexico and America. Her favorite food is pancakes.

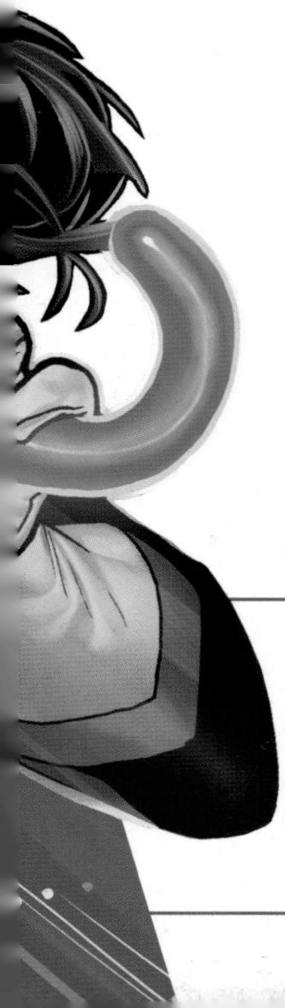

DATA FILE

Friends and allies: Star Sapphire (p26), Soranik Natu (p90)

Base: Portland, OR

Enemies: Sinestro, Darkseid

CATWOMAN

"No one would ever mistake me for a hero, but I do have some standards."

Selina Kyle is an expert burglar and master thief known in Gotham City as Catwoman. As an orphaned and penniless child, Selina became a thief to survive. She is deadly silent in her black catsuit and mask—entering buildings without a sound and leaving no trace behind. Selina is also a master martial artist and carries a whip with her for protection in case of danger.

Catwoman has stolen everything from fancy cars to priceless diamonds from Gotham City's most wealthy and dishonest citizens. Now, she has mostly given up her life of crime to work alongside Batman and other Super Heroes. She has been a member of both the Justice League of America and the Birds of Prey teams. Selina may not always do the right thing—but when she does the wrong thing, it is usually for the right reasons, like helping those in need. She is very good at convincing people to do what she wants them to do.

DATA FILE

Friends and allies: Katana (p44), Stargirl (p48)
Special skill: Fluent in Mandarin
Loves: Her sharp, retractable claws

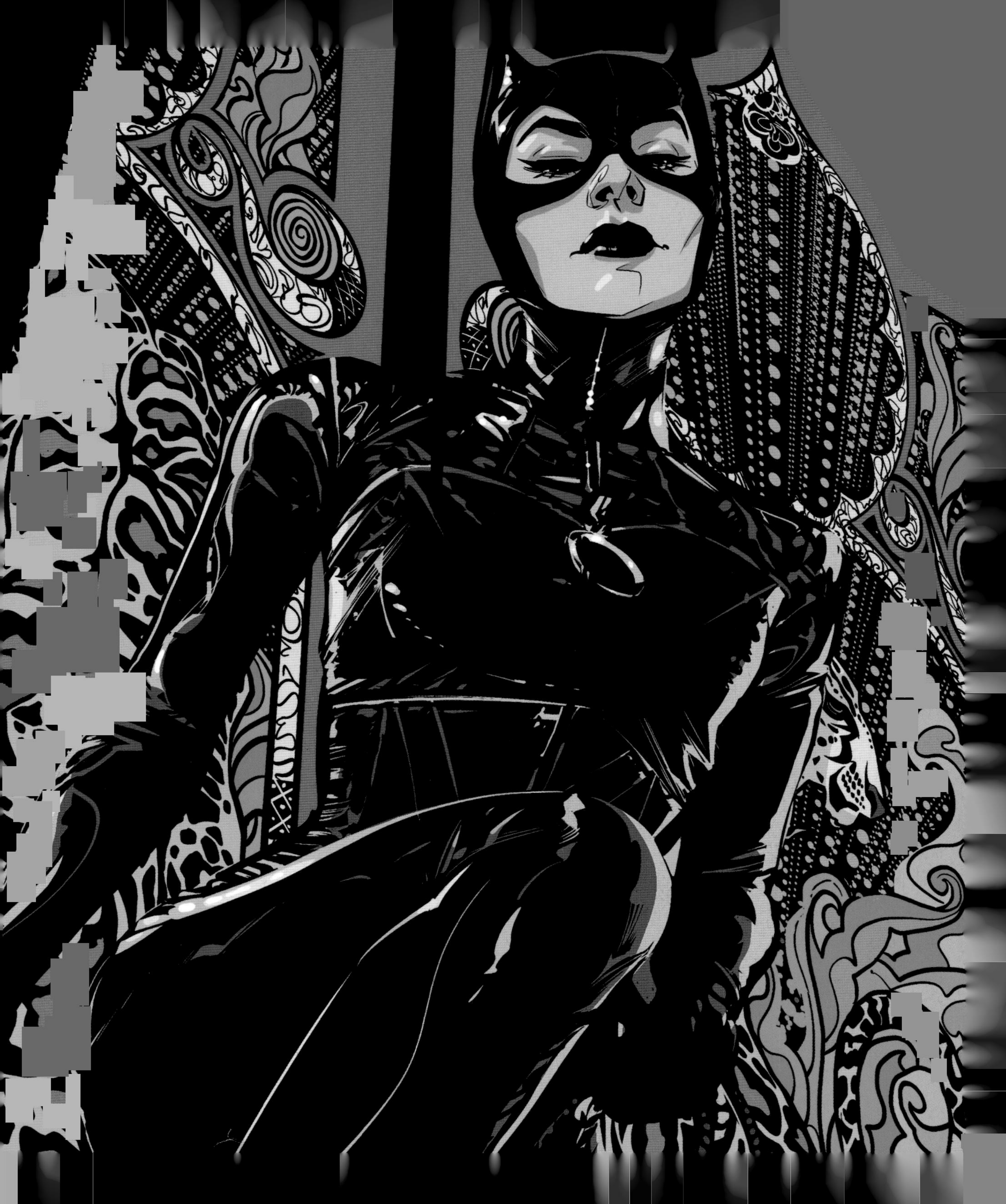

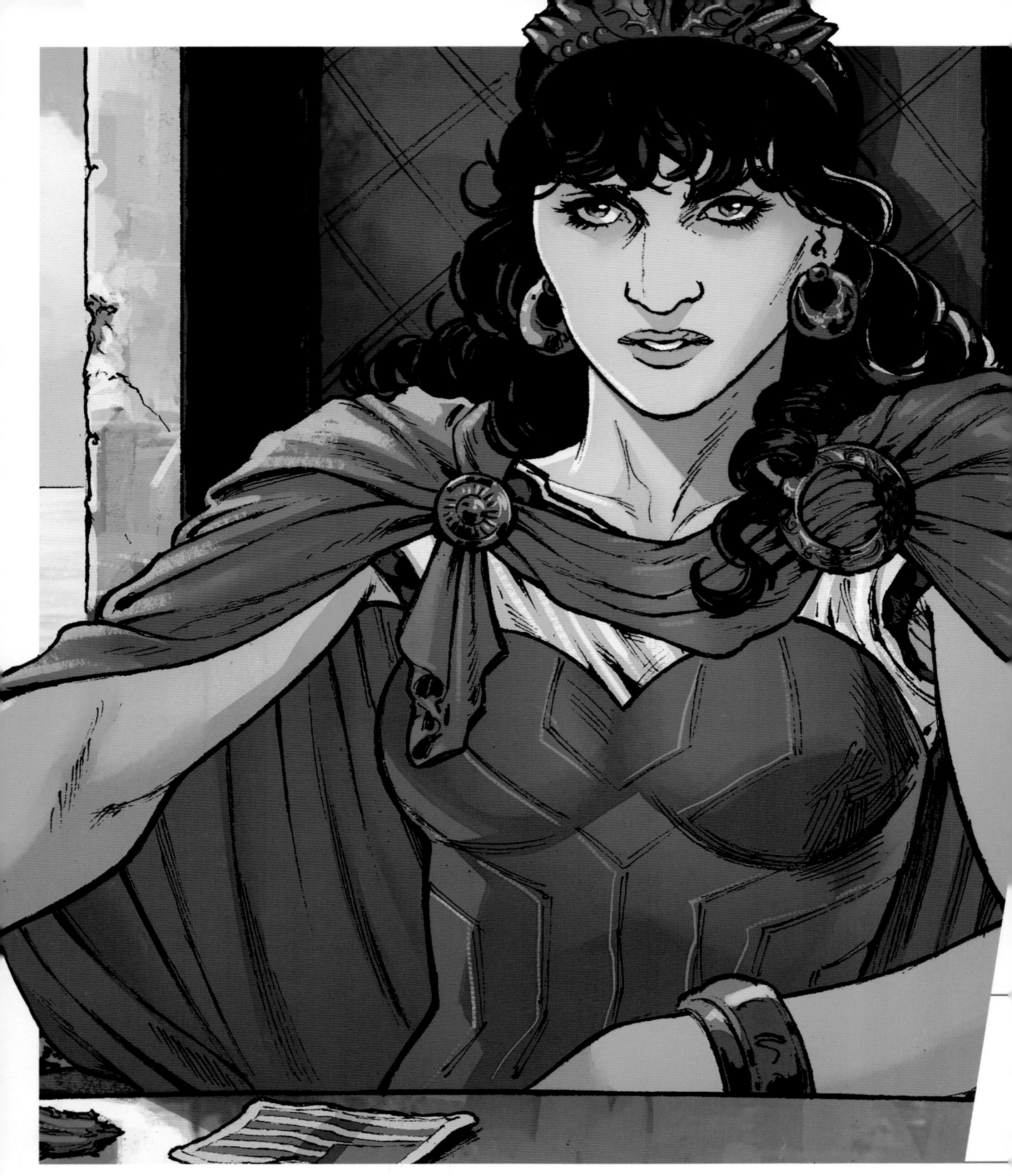

HIPPOLYTA

"My daughter... you always make me proud..."

Hippolyta is a powerful and immortal ruler. She has reigned as queen and leader of the Amazons of Themyscira for 3,000 years. With all these centuries of training behind her, Hippolyta is nearly undefeatable in combat. She can bend steel with her bare hands (though she prefers to fight with a broadsword and shield). She is also a shining example of the Amazons' dedication to peace and equality.

When a human washed up on Themyscira's shores, it was Hippolyta who began a competition to see which Amazon would return him to the mortal world. She did this even though she knew that her own daughter, Diana, would probably win, and so volunteer to leave Themyscira and Hippolyta forever. If Diana were to return to her mother, the violent God of War Ares would be released from his eternal prison. Though Diana can never come back home, Hippolyta is incredibly proud of her daughter and her choice to protect humanity from danger.

DATA FILE

Friends and allies: Wonder Woman (p12), Artemis (p106)
Loves: Swordfighting, her Amazons
Special skills: Archery, horseback riding

STARFIRE

"I said I'd **never** let them **beat me.** They **never did...** and they **never will!"**

Koriand'r is a princess from the planet Tamaran. Like all Tamaraneans, Kory has orange skin that absorbs ultraviolet (UV) radiation from stars. She uses this UV power to fly. Betrayed by her own scheming sister, Kory was kidnapped by an evil alien race who carried out experiments on her. These experiments increased Kory's natural powers and also gave her the ability to shoot concentrated blasts of solar power called starbolts from her hands. Koriand'r used her new powers to overthrow her captors and restore order to Tamaran.

Optimistic, reliable, and honest, Kory is famous throughout the galaxy as the Tamaranean hero Starfire. She headed to Earth to fight for those in need, and joined forces with Super Hero group the Teen Titans. She eventually became their leader. Kory is now a member of Justice League Odyssey, alongside other space-traveling heroes like Green Lantern Jessica Cruz. In her spare time, Kory likes to look after her garden.

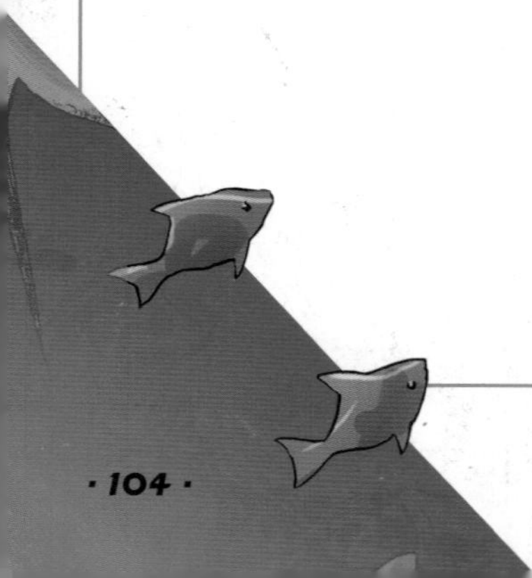

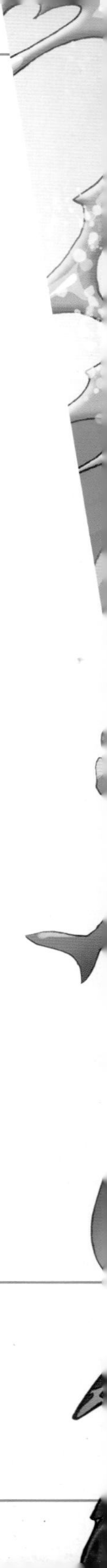

DATA FILE

Friends and allies: Dove (p20), Emiko Queen (p116)
Special skills: Spaceship piloting, modeling
Enemies: The Citadel, Trigon

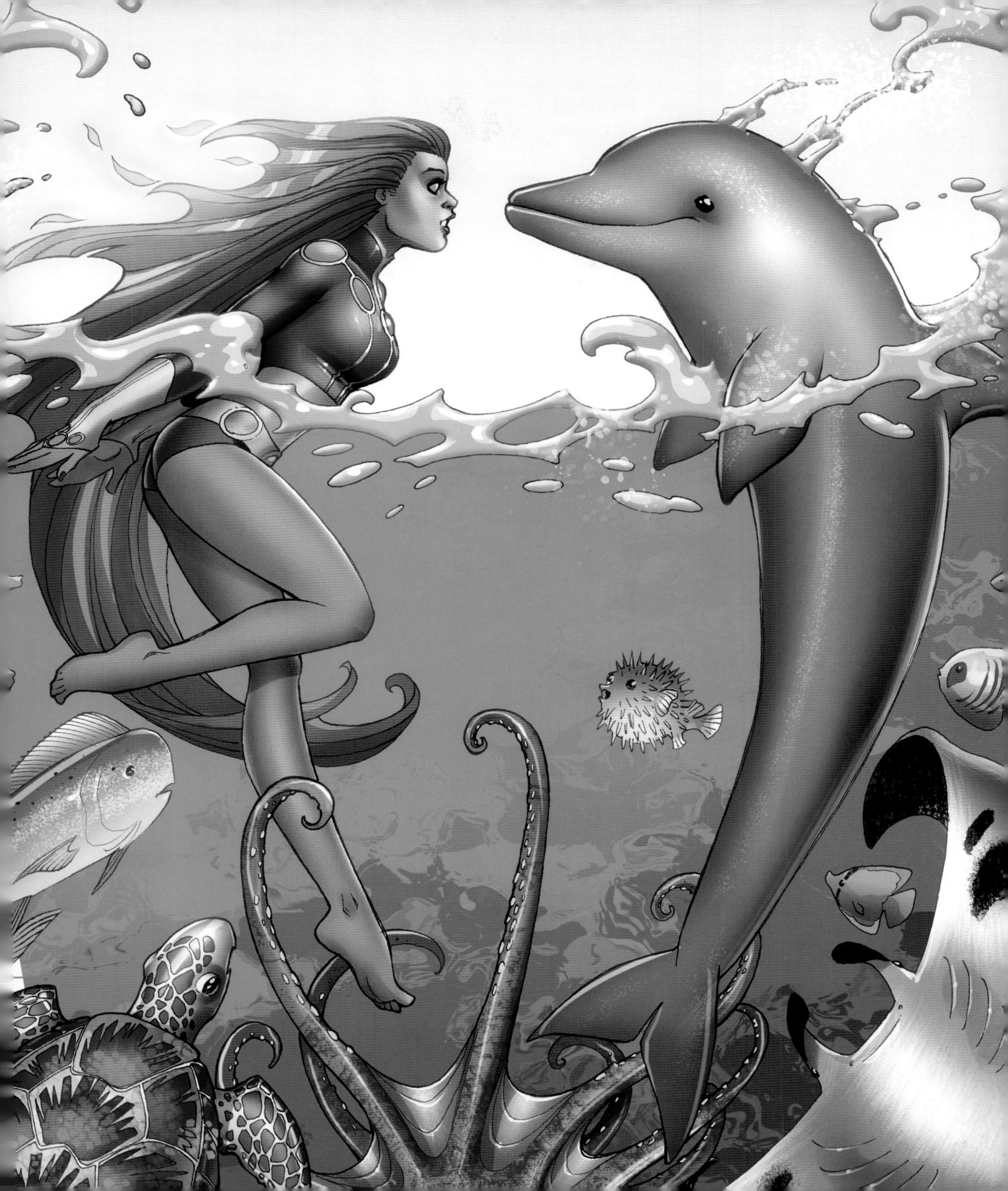

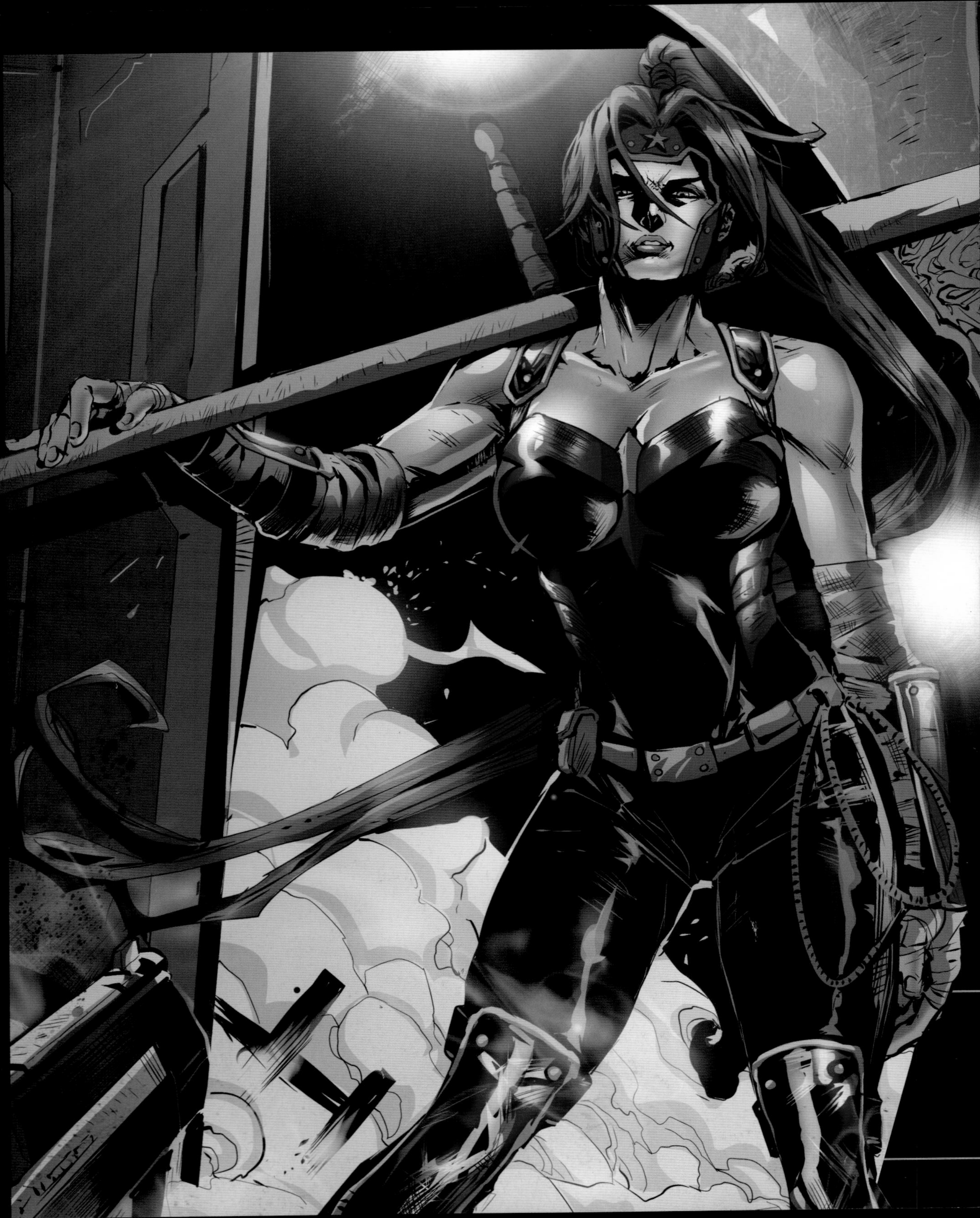

ARTEMIS

"To be crystal clear going forward—do not—call me—princess."

Over 3,000 years ago, a small band of Amazon warriors left their home island of Themyscira. They settled in ancient Egypt. Artemis was one of these immortal Amazons. She helped build their new city, Bana-Mighdall, which means "The Temple of Women." Their city was protected by goddesses of many different religions.

Fierce Artemis is the strongest of her kind. She was once the Shim'Tar (champion warrior) of the Amazons of Bana-Mighdall and wielded their most powerful weapon, the Bow of Ra. To protect the rest of the world, Artemis gave up her title, returned the bow to her tribe, and traveled to Gotham City. Her best friend, Akila, became the Shim'Tar in her place. In Gotham City, Artemis joined forces with Red Hood (who previously went by the Super Hero name Robin) and Bizarro (a clone of Superman). This odd trio formed a team known as the Outlaws and together they fight evil. Artemis now uses a giant battle ax with divine power that she calls "Mistress."

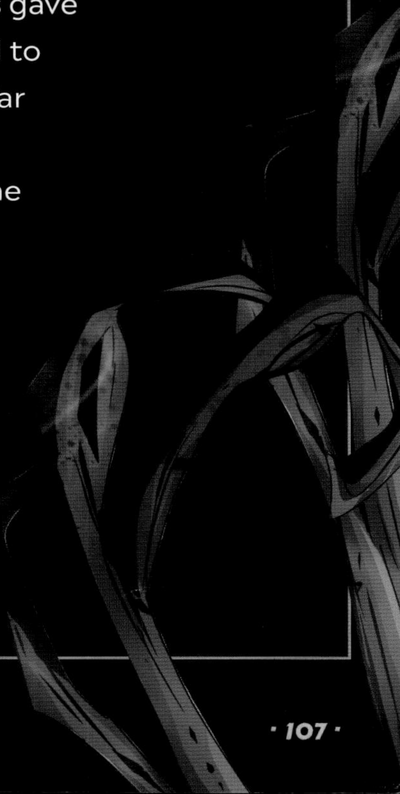

DATA FILE

Friends and allies: Wonder Woman (p12), Hippolyta (p102)
Base: Gotham City
Loves: Gleaming weapons

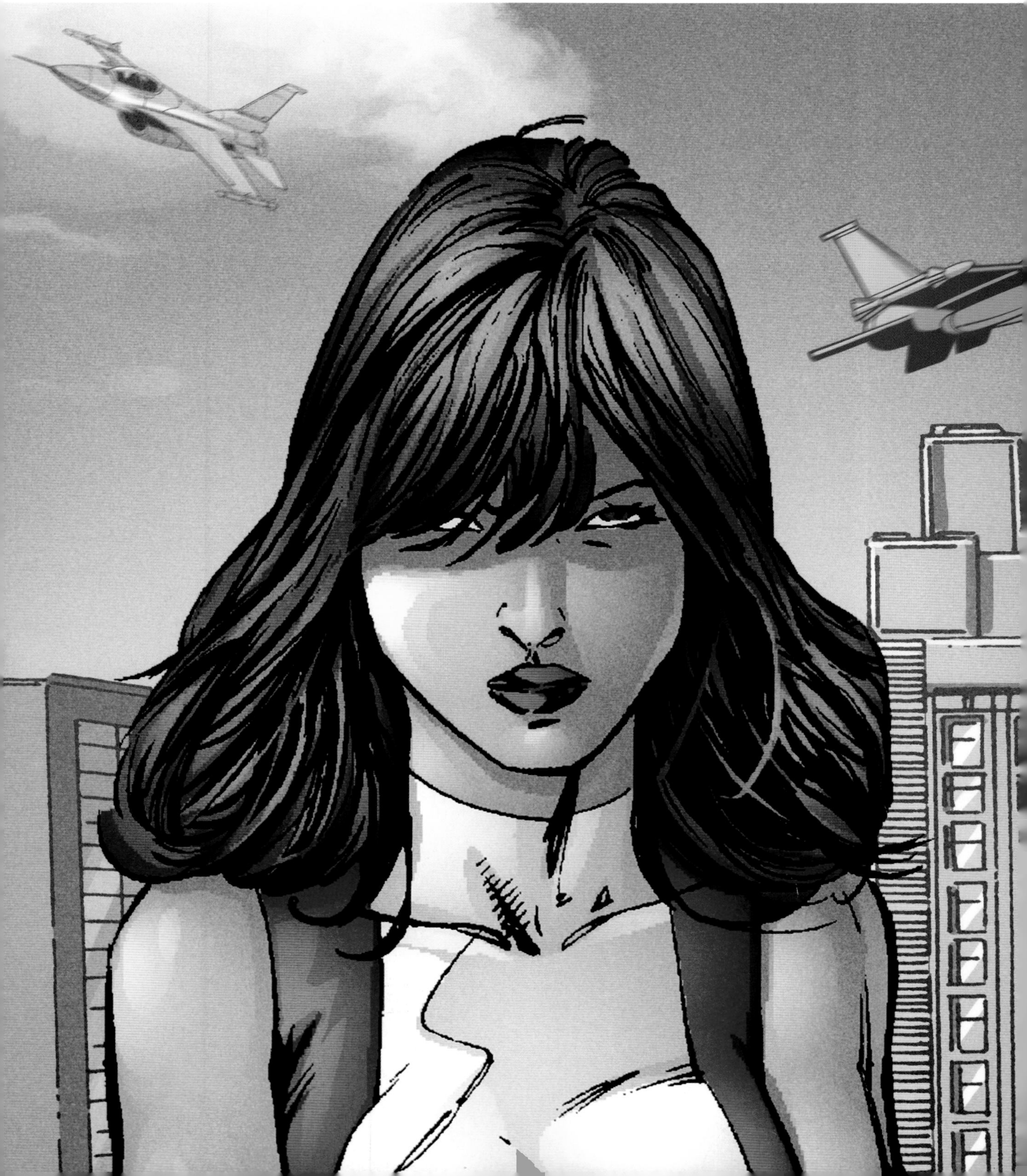

ELASTI-WOMAN

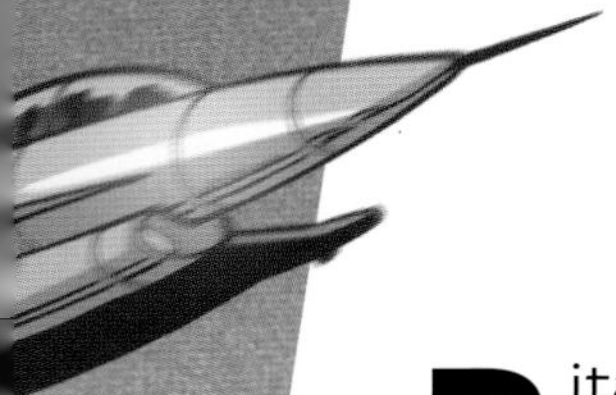

"Every day in every way I'm getting better and better."

Rita Farr was an Olympic gold medalist in swimming and a successful Hollywood horror movie actress. While she was on a film shoot in Africa, she was exposed to mysterious volcanic gases. Afterward, Rita was able to grow as large as a skyscraper or shrink as small as a bug. Unable to control her new abilities, Rita's acting career was over. But, brave and determined as she always is, Rita decided to make the very best of her new life.

Rita was recruited by scientist Dr. Niles Caulder to become part of the Doom Patrol, a team of outcasts with superpowers. She took the new name Elasti-Woman. Rita trained hard and eventually gained enough control over her powers to grow or shrink individual body parts at will. Rita married her Doom Patrol teammate Steve Dayton (the Super Hero Mento) and adopted Beast Boy, a member of the Teen Titans. When Rita sleeps, she loses control over her body and turns into a puddle.

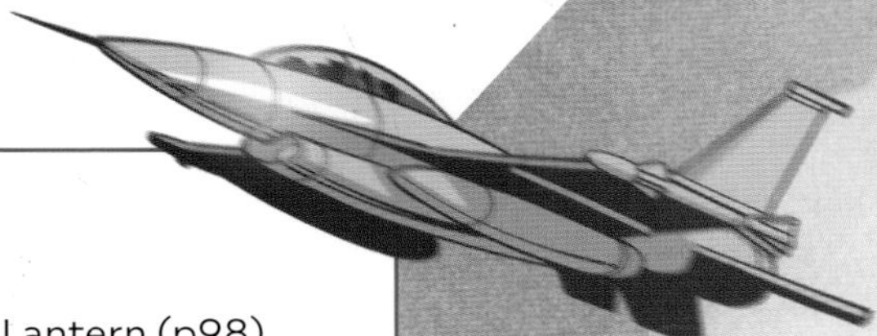

DATA FILE

Friends and allies: Bumblebee (p36), Green Lantern (p98)

Loves: Drama

Base: Doom Patrol HQ, MI

RAVEN

"I can give back without being paid."

Raven is a member of the Teen Titans. Her father is a powerful, interdimensional demon. Raven's human mother ran away with her to hide in the mystical dimension Azarath, where Raven could avoid her evil father's influence. When she eventually learned the truth about her heritage as a teenager, she fled to Earth. Raven formed a close bond with Beast Boy, a member of the Teen Titans, who introduced her to the rest of the team.

Despite Raven's dark past and the potential for evil in her blood, the Titans love and accept her. She must keep a strong hold on her own emotions to keep her demon side at bay. Raven is an empath, able to sense and control other people's emotions and thoughts. In fights, Raven projects her "Soul-Self," a spirit that can teleport, fly, travel through time, and become intangible. Raven is fiercely protective of her Titan friends. She uses the name Rachel Roth as a civilian on Earth and, probably unsurprisingly, she likes Goth fashion.

DATA FILE

Friends and allies: Donna Troy (p62), Starfire (p104)
Enemy: The darkness within her
Special skill: Can sometimes see the future

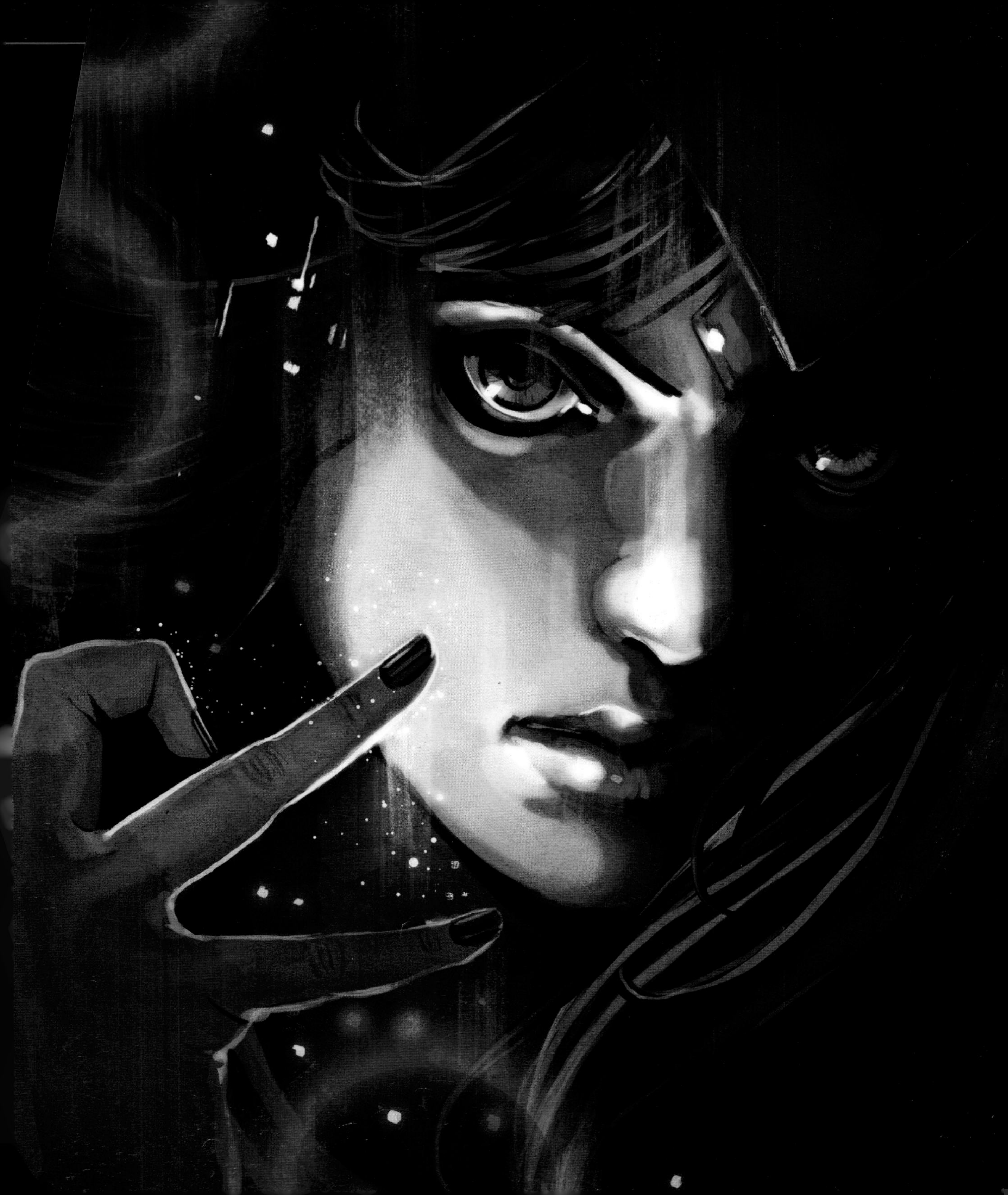

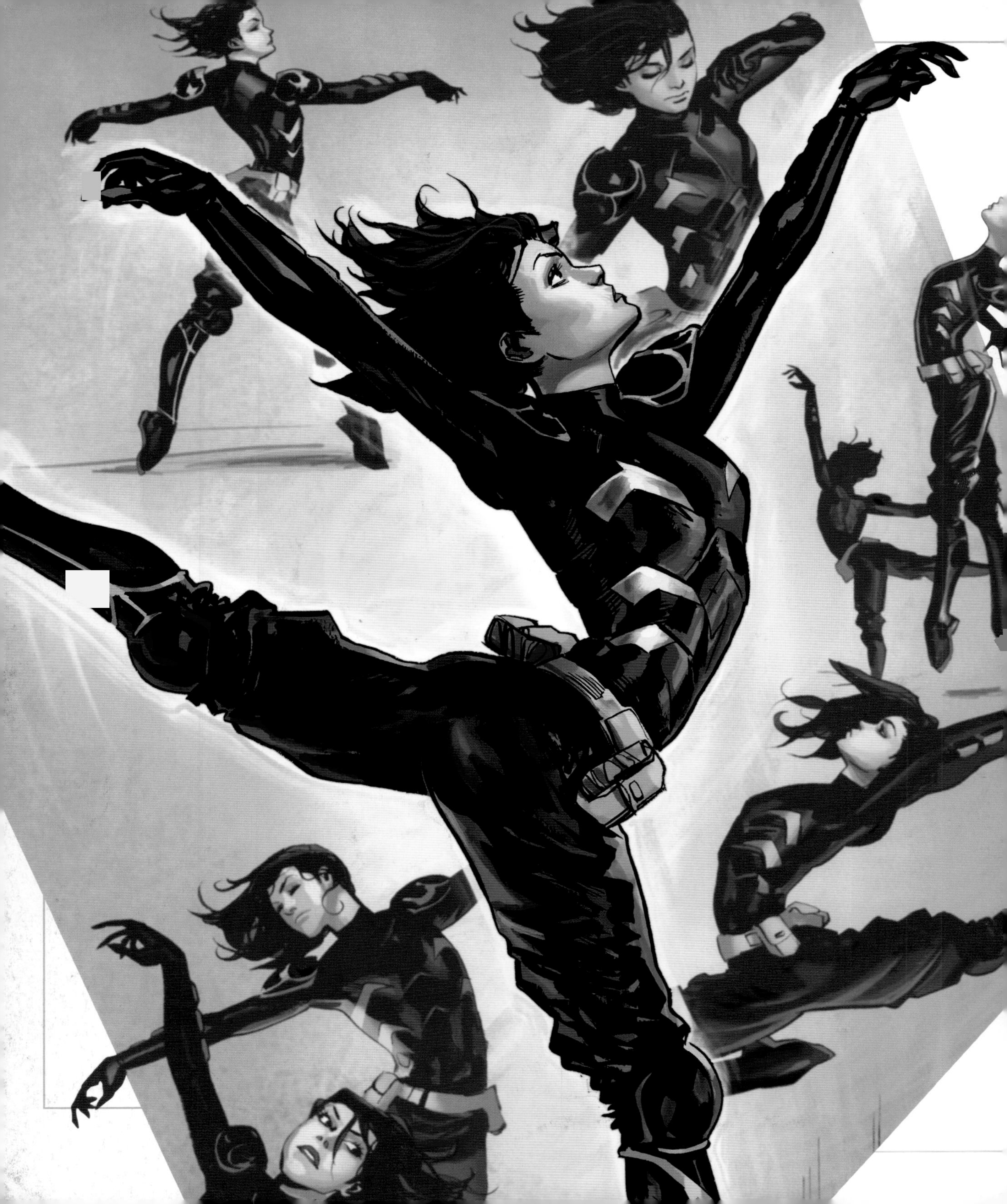

ORPHAN

"Don't worry. I'm... a **detective.**"

Cassandra Cain was raised to be a human weapon. Her parents were both assassins and wanted their daughter to follow in their footsteps. They did not teach Cassandra how to read or write. Instead, they taught her only how to read body language so she could become a skilled fighter. Cassandra managed to escape her parents and ran away to Gotham City. The Super Hero Batman saw past Cassandra's communication challenges and brought her into his group of crime fighters.

Cassandra took on her father's former code name, Orphan. She uses her skills to help others instead of doing harm. Cassandra joined Batwoman's bootcamp for young Super Heroes with her new friend Stephanie Brown (the crime fighter Spoiler). She is now learning how to protect Gotham City in the best way. Because of her extreme upbringing, Cassandra can immediately spot a person's weaknesses and figure out how to beat them in combat. She is still figuring out how to socialize.

DATA FILE

Friends and allies: Bluebird (p88), Spoiler (p118)
Base: The Belfry, Gotham City
Enemies: The League of Shadows, dyslexia

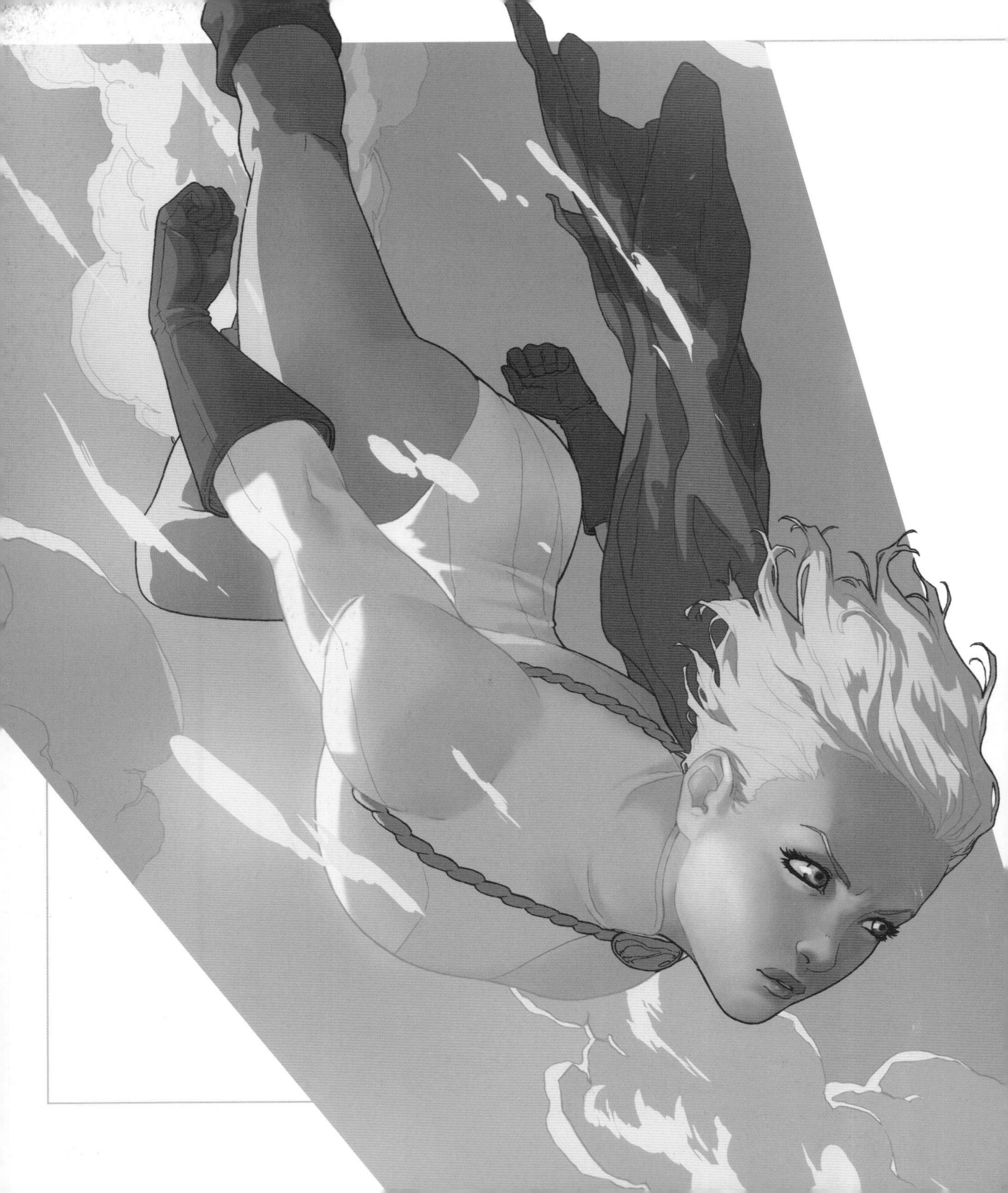

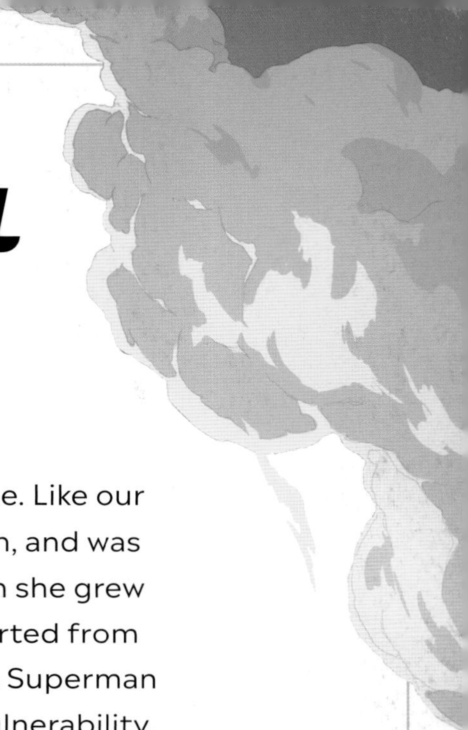

POWER GIRL

"It's not every day I get to rescue myself."

Kara Zor-L is Supergirl from an alternate universe. Like our universe's Kara Zor-El, she is Superman's cousin, and was sent to Earth from her home planet, Krypton. When she grew up, a cosmic event caused Kara Zor-L to be transported from her Earth to our Earth. She has the same powers as Superman and our Earth's Supergirl—strength, flight, and invulnerability, to name a few. She now protects humanity as Power Girl, wanting to create her own unique identity.

Power Girl goes by the human name Karen Starr when she wants to disguise herself. Her different life experiences have made Karen more mature emotionally than Supergirl. Karen now runs Starr Enterprises, combining her love of both business and science. Her company develops technology that Karen hopes might be able to send her back to her own Earth one day. Far away from her own friends and family, Karen has made the most of her new home and new allies in the Justice Society of America.

DATA FILE

Friends and allies: Supergirl (p32), Huntress (p40)

Loves: Business management, capes

Base: Brooklyn, NY

EMIKO QUEEN

"We can't be stuck in the past forever, right?"

Emiko Queen is a crime fighter and a master of the bow and arrow. Her mother is the infamous assassin Shado and her father was the super-rich businessman Robert Queen. Emiko also has a half brother: Oliver Queen, the heroic archer known as Green Arrow. Emiko was kidnapped as a child. She was raised and trained by one of her father's enemies. When Emiko learned about her real family, she joined forces with her older half brother to fight crime. Oliver has said that Emi is even better at archery than he is.

Emiko goes by the Super Hero name Red Arrow and helps protect her city from evildoers. She often works alongside Green Arrow, Black Canary, and the Seattle Police Department. Emi is also skilled in acrobatics, martial arts, and stealth combat. She is now a member of the Teen Titans, the teenage Super Heroes who help defeat the evil forces that plague the Earth. Emi and Oliver argue as often as most stubborn siblings do. Emi is usually right.

DATA FILE
Friends and allies: The Flash of China (p52), Crush (p68)
Base: Seattle, WA
Place of birth: Starfish Island, Fiji

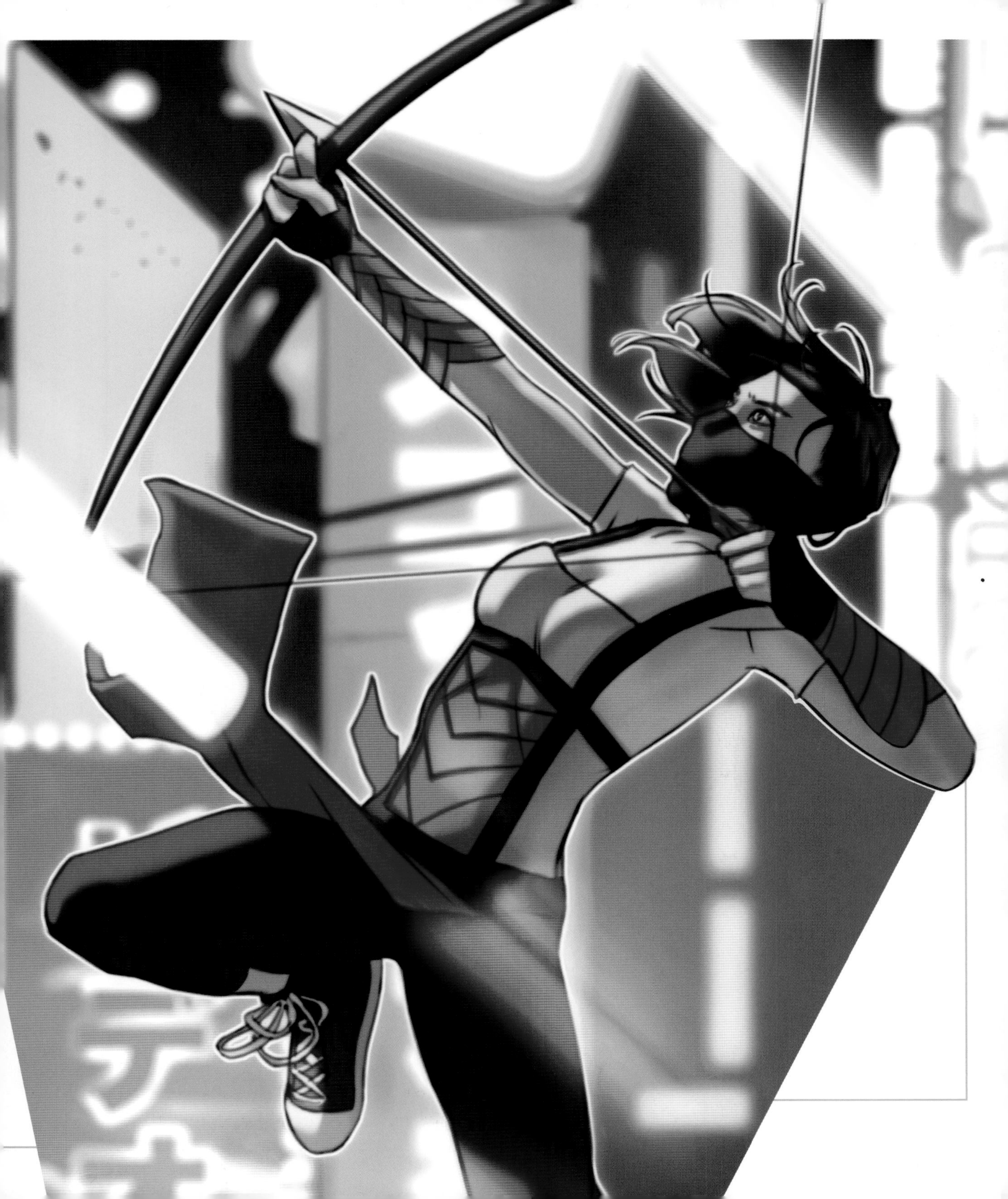

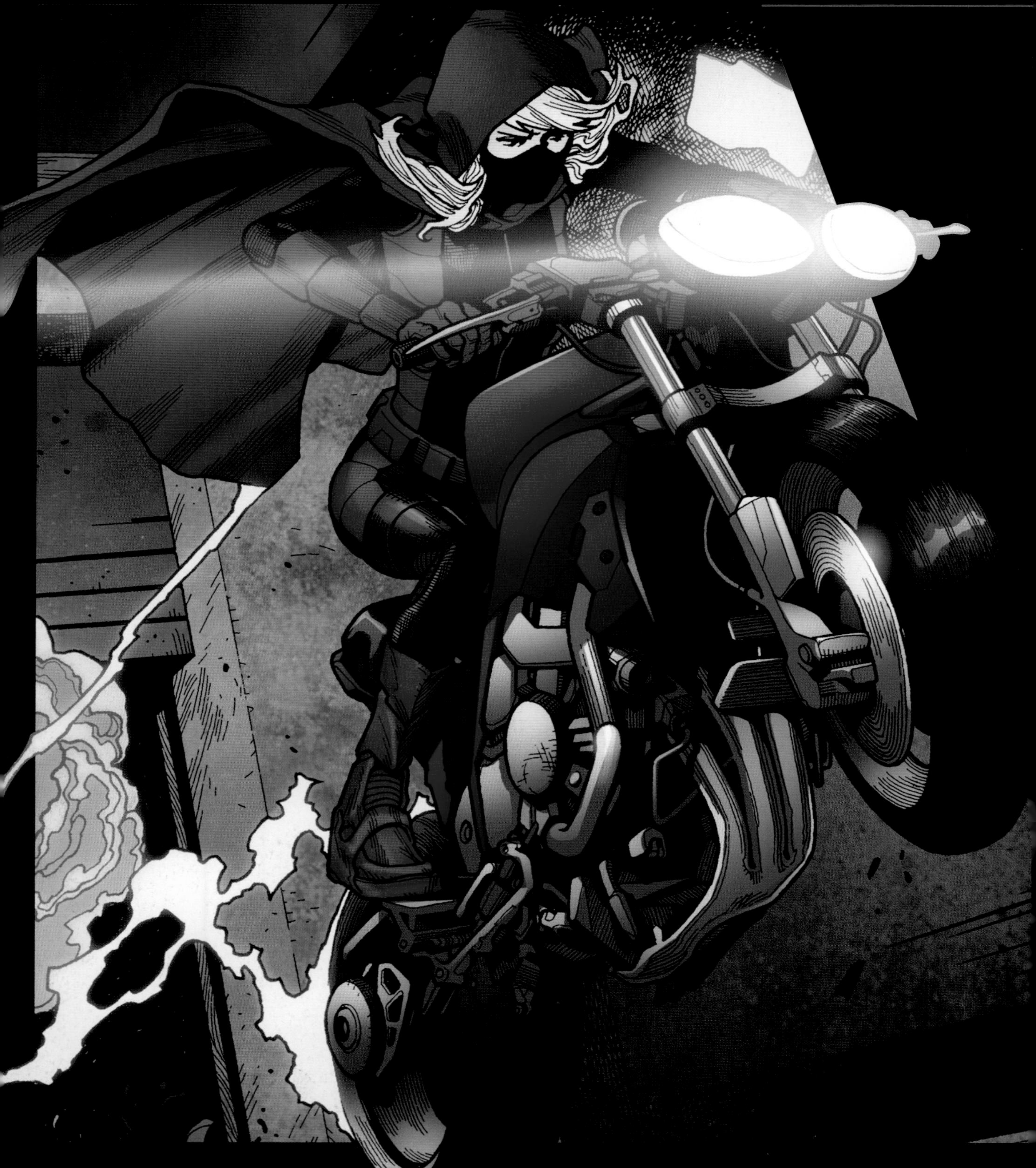

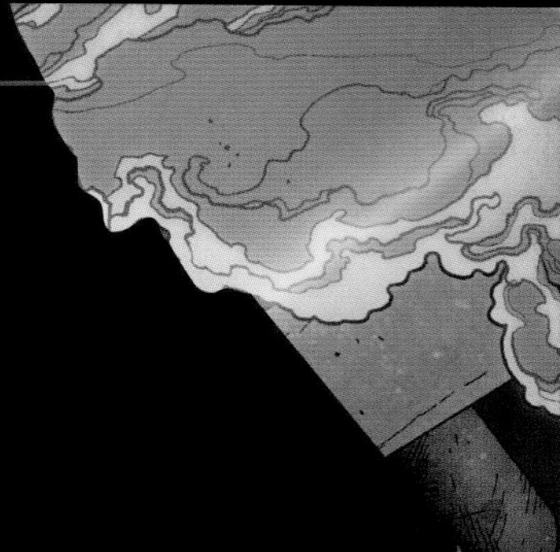

SPOILER

"I'm almost fifty percent sure nothing could go wrong."

Stephanie Brown was raised without knowing her father's secret identity. He was the Cluemaster, a former game show host, who became a super-villain and terrorized Gotham City. When Stephanie learned the truth about her father, she rebelled against him and decided to make up for his evil acts. With a cape and two blunt batons called Eskrima sticks, Stephanie began fighting crime as Spoiler—because she vowed to spoil any villains' evil plans.

Stephanie received training from Batgirl, Catwoman, and the Birds of Prey group. She is especially good at martial arts and motorcycle riding. Alongside the crime fighter Orphan, Stephanie is now a part of Batwoman's emergency response team in Gotham City. She is dating Tim Drake, also known as the Super Hero Red Robin. Stephanie loves sarcastic one-liners and waffles. She wants people to know that her costume is technically the color "eggplant" and definitely not "purple."

DATA FILE

Friends and allies: Batwoman (p96), Orphan (p112)

Base: The Belfry, Gotham City

Special skills: Playing the piano, computer hacking

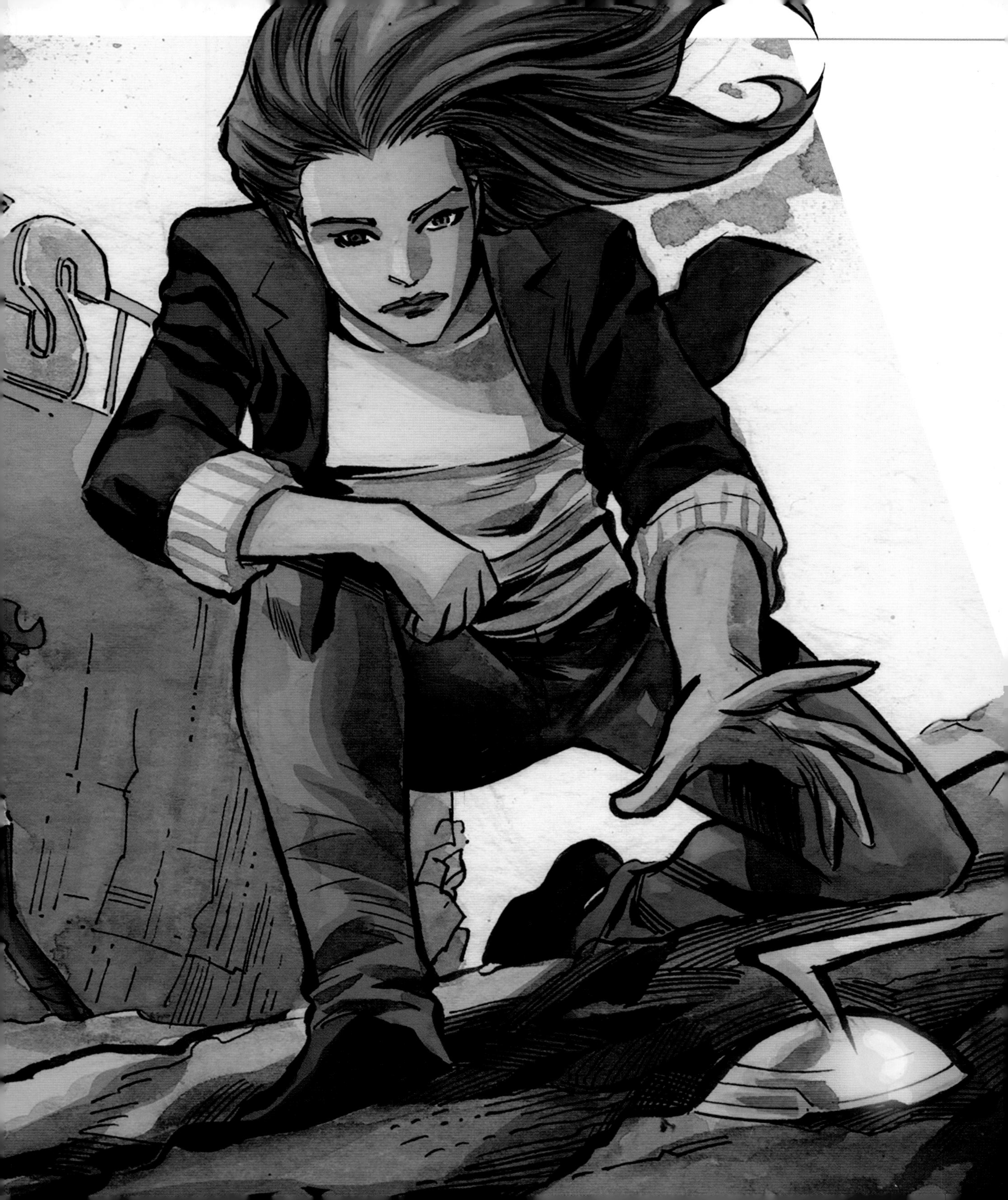

IRIS WEST

"You can't **turn your back** on anyone who's really **hurting.**"

Iris West is one of Central City's most talented reporters. After interning for the *Gotham Gazette* newspaper in Gotham City, Iris joined the *Central City Picture News* as an investigative journalist. She often came into contact with Barry Allen, a forensic scientist for the Central City Police Department. What Iris did not know was that Barry Allen was actually the alter ego of The Flash—the very Super Hero whose identity she aimed to reveal in a newspaper article.

While reporting, Iris has met and helped many of the superpowered heroes working out of S.T.A.R. Labs. Even her own nephew, Wallace West, has speedster powers like The Flash. In an alternate timeline, Iris was married to Barry Allen, and she has some buried memories of this alternate reality. Though Iris has no superpowers, she is strong-willed, tough, and driven. She may face tricky adventures with time travel, cosmic energy, super-villains, and speedsters, but her determination never wavers.

DATA FILE

Friends and allies: The Flash of China (p52), Emiko Queen (p116)
Loves: Photography, investigation
Enemies: Reverse-Flash, Gorilla Grodd

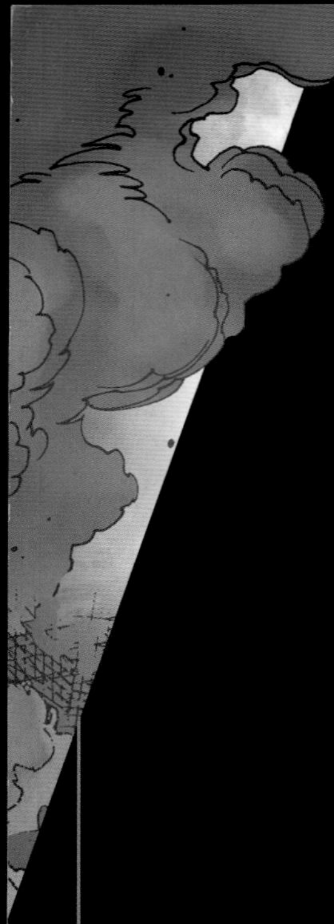

PHANTOM GIRL

"Don't worry, boss. I got this."

Linnya Wazzo is from an alternate-dimension version of Earth called Bgztl. On Bgztl, all people can make their bodies intangible. They can phase through solid objects like phantoms. When she was a child, a space-travel accident trapped Linnya in a scary dimension known as the Dark Multiverse. While stuck in the Dark Multiverse, Linnya became permanently intangible.

Linnya was discovered by the three Super Heroes Metamorpho, Mr. Terrific, and Plastic Man. She returned to our Earth with them and took on the name Phantom Girl. Together they formed a Super Hero squad named The Terrifics. In our universe, Linnya can make her body solid again—but anything she touches while she is solid explodes. She is working with Mr. Terrific to cure her condition, and to fight against the evil forces of the Dark Multiverse. Linnya always stays cheerful and optimistic, and tries hard to find her confidence in dangerous situations. She writes about life in her own intangible ghost diary.

DATA FILE

Friends and allies: Saturn Girl (p24), Supergirl (p32)

Loves: Her family, giant spiders

Enemies: Evildoers from the Dark Multiverse

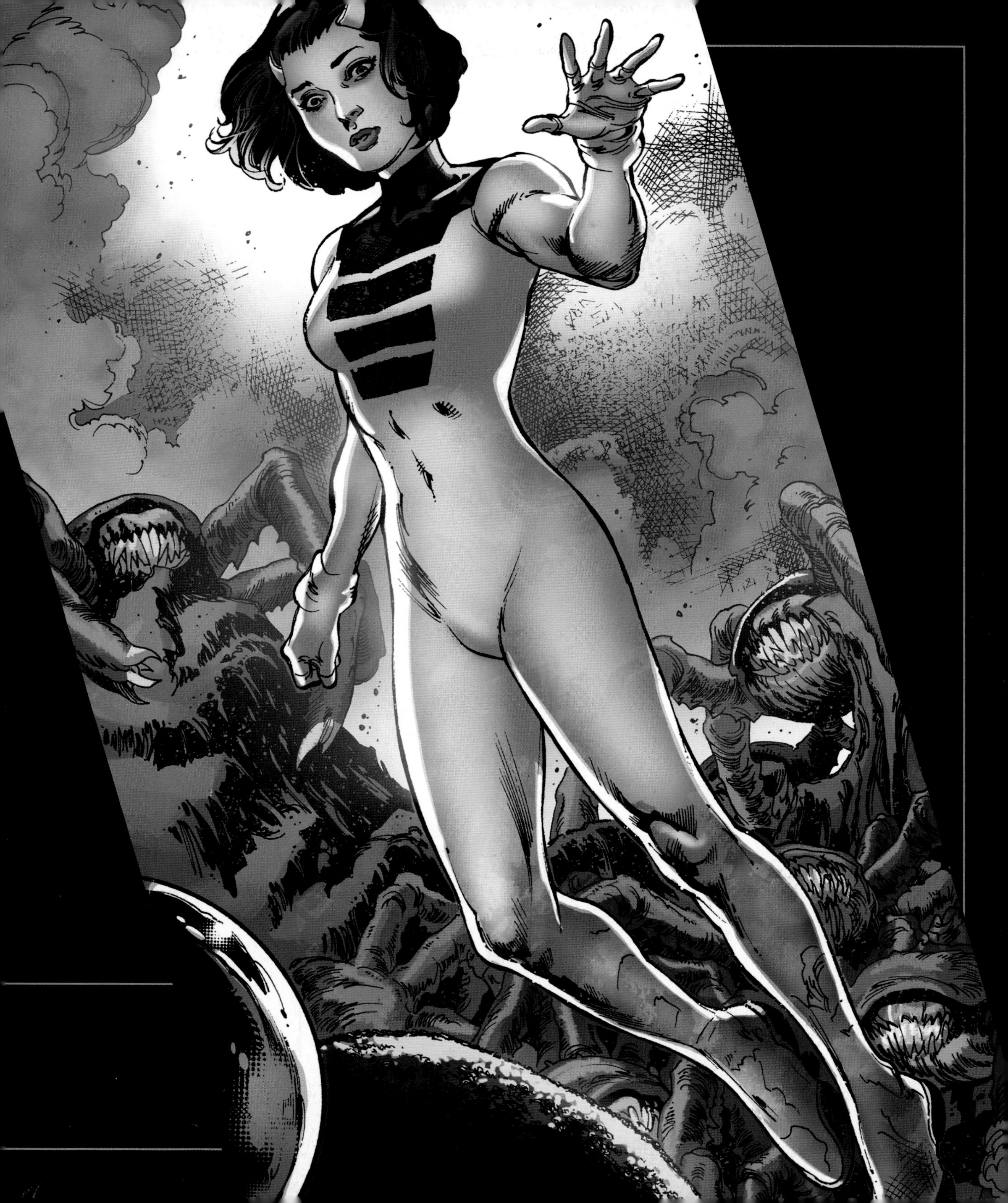

GLOSSARY

alliance: an agreement between different people or groups to work together.

alter ego: a side of somebody's personality that is different, such as a secret identity.

antihero: a central character who lacks the traditional values of a hero like goodness and honor.

artifacts: objects that are of cultural or historic interest.

broadsword: a large, heavy sword with a wide blade.

civil war: a war between different groups of people who live in the same country.

cosmic: something that comes not from Earth but from the universe.

density: a measurement to describe how compact an object is—the amount of space it fills compared to the amount of stuff it contains.

devastated: extremely upset or shocked.

dimension: a world or universe.

durable: tough or resistant.

empathy: the ability to understand and feel, or share, others' emotions.

engulfing: covering or surrounding.

extra-dimensional: beyond or outside of our own dimension.

forensic: using scientific methods to solve crime.

formation: creation or development.

immortal: a living being who will never die and live forever.

impulsive: when a person reacts or takes action quickly without thinking first.

incarnation: the physical form or body taken by the spirit of another person or god.

infamous: being well-known for an evil quality or action.

intangible: someone or something that cannot be touched or grasped.

interdimensional: between dimensions.

invulnerable: impossible to wound or destroy.

jumper cables: long, electric cables used to connect a battery to a vehicle's engine temporarily.

kinetic: related to motion or movement.

magnitude: the size or extent of something.

manipulate: control or handle with skill.

mortal: a living being who does not live forever and will die.

nervous system: a network of nerves and cells that allows different parts of the body to communicate, including the brain and spinal cord.

neurosurgeon: a doctor who carries out operations on the nervous system.

one-liners: short, witty jokes.

outcasts: people who are excluded or rejected from their communities.

overcome: defeat or conquer.

GLOSSARY (CONTINUED)

parasite: something that survives by living inside or on another living thing.

Pegasus: a winged horse.

PhD: short for "Doctor of Philosophy"—the highest degree awarded by a university.

plucky: daring or spirited.

post-doctoral fellowship: a period of professional study or research taken by a person who has finished their PhD.

phase: pass through a solid object.

radioactive: having or producing a powerful and dangerous form of energy named radiation.

reserved: quiet or private; someone who does not reveal their own feelings or thoughts.

rival: enemy or foe.

shards: small, hard, sharp pieces or fragments of something.

stamina: long-lasting energy.

supersonic: faster than the speed of sound.

teleportation: traveling across space or dimensions in an instant.

undercut: a hairstyle in which a section of the hair is shaved close to the head.

willpower: determination to do something.

yielded: gave up an argument or fight; admitted defeat to another person.

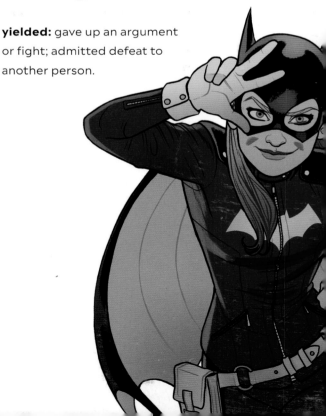

ARTIST ACKNOWLEDGMENTS

Laura Allred, Brad Anderson, Michael Atiyeh, Sami Basri, Blond, Viktor Bogdanovic, Brian Bolland, Brett Booth, Geraldo Borges, Corey Breen, Brian Buccellato, Jamal Campbell, Eleonora Carlini, Cliff Chiang, Matthew Clark, Andy Clarke, Amanda Conner, Kevin Conrad, Andrew Dalhouse, Tony S. Daniel, John Dell, Taylor Esposito, Romulo Fajardo, Jr., Wayne Faucher, Juan Ferreyra, David Finch, W. Scott Forbes, Gary Frank, Jenny Frison, Veronica Gandini, Sunny Gho, Jonathan Glapion, Patrick Gleason, Ian Hannin, Stephanie Hans, Doug Hazlewood, Daniel Henriques, Ian Herring, Hi-Fi, Matt Hollingsworth, Sandra Hope, Richard Horie, Tanya Horie, Adam Hughes, Joëlle Jones, Minkyu Jung, Dan Jurgens, John Kalisz, Scott Kolins, Travis Lanham, Serge LaPointe, Jim Lee, Rob Leigh, Aaron Lopresti, Warren Louw, Adriano Lucas, Emanuela Lupacchino, Kevin Maguire, Marcelo Maiolo, Guy Major, Francis Manapul, Clay Mann, Guillem March, Laura Martin, Francesco Mattina, Ray McCarthy, Mike McKone, Joshua Middleton, Tomeu Morey, Paul Mounts, Sean Murphy, Steve Oliff, George Pérez, Joe Prado, Joe Quinones, Wil Quintana, Ron Randall, Norm Rapmund, Bruno Redondo, Josh Reed, Ivan Reis, Ricken, Robson Rocha, Alex Ross, Stéphane Roux, Joe Rubinstein, Alejandro Sanchez, Nicola Scott, Stephen Segovia, Stjepan Sejic, Liam Sharp, Paulo Siqueira, Dexter Soy, Mike Spicer, Cameron Stewart, Marcio Takara, Philip Tan, Babs Tarr, Art Thibert, Ethan Van Sciver, Robert Venditti, Steve Wands, Dean White, and J.H. Williams III

The publishers have made every effort to identify and acknowledge the artists whose work appears in this book.

Senior Editor Ruth Amos
Senior Designer Clive Savage
Designer Rosamund Bird
Pre-Production Producer Marc Staples
Senior Producer Mary Slater
Managing Editor Sadie Smith
Managing Art Editor Vicky Short
Publisher Julie Ferris
Art Director Lisa Lanzarini
Publishing Director Simon Beecroft

Cover artists Emanuela Lupacchino, Brett Breeding, and Tomeu Morey

DK would like to thank Jon Hall, Sam Bartlett, and Jessica Tapolcai
for design assistance; Shari Last for editorial assistance;
and Megan Douglass for proofreading.

First American Edition, 2019
Published in the United States by DK Publishing
1450 Broadway, Suite 801, New York, New York 10018

Page design copyright © 2019 Dorling Kindersley Limited
DK, a Division of Penguin Random House LLC
19 20 21 22 23 10 9 8 7 6 5 4 3 2 1
001-314866-Dec/2019

A catalog record for this book is available from the Library of Congress.

ISBN 978-1-4654-8611-0

DK books are available at special discounts when purchased in bulk for sales promotions, premiums,
fund-raising, or educational use. For details, contact: DK Publishing Special Markets,
1450 Broadway, Suite 801, New York, New York 10018
SpecialSales@dk.com

Printed and bound in China

A WORLD OF IDEAS:
SEE ALL THERE IS TO KNOW

www.dk.com
www.dccomics.com